# THE HUNCHBACK

*Dark Tales*

## REGINE ABEL

**Cover by**
Regine Abel

**Art By**
Astor Alexander
Sam Griffin
Muns

**Copyright © 2019**

# CONTENTS

# THE HUNCHBACK

**Her heart's desire would be her downfall.**

After spending her life in training, Esmeralda still can't believe she's been appointed to serve as the Vestal of Our Lady of Paris —the greatest temple on any planet in the Nine Circles. Her beauty and unrivaled ability to manipulate energy quickly catch the attention of Praetor Frollo, the grand magistrate of Paris, and High Seraph Phoebus, the greatest winged warrior in the solar system. But her dream of becoming the consort of one of those handsome, powerful males is forgotten the moment she lays eyes upon the hunchback secretly living in the temple.

Kwazeem feels Esmeralda's power as soon as she lands in his city. She awakens the primal energy that has lain dormant within him—and a possessive hunger that demands he claim her. But he's a Fallen, a monster that would be destroyed on sight if the citizens of Paris discovered his existence. Worse still, Esmeralda's Divine Light inflicts agony upon his already tortured body if he basks in it for too long. And yet... he cannot stay away from her.

With Kwazeem's mysterious condition and Esmeralda torn between her duties to the people and the sinful desires of her heart, is there any chance of them sharing a future?

# DEDICATION

*To the wondrous imagination of the authors of old who brought us the fairy tales, folktales, and fables that filled our youth with magic. To every prince and princess inside all of us who ever dreamed of their happily ever after. To anyone who fought and continues to fight for the right to love the chosen of their heart, no matter what hurdles get thrown in their paths.*

*To Melissa Stewart for being a classy lady and for going above and beyond to help me get this book out properly.*

*To my family, love you always.*

## CHAPTER 1
KWAZEEM

I opened the window to let the sun shine into the room and over my miserable existence. The frame glowed with a soft, white light, as did many things in Paris: the City of Lights. Turning around, I cast a final look at the sumptuous bedroom to make sure everything was in order. Praetor Frollo would give me an earful if I mucked things up.

With heavy steps, I approached the massive bed to fix the light-blue sheets embroidered with lumis which covered it. The fine, luminous thread adjusted its glow to the brightness of the room or to voice commands. Currently at minimum dimness, it made it harder to notice that the pattern in the right corner wasn't perfectly aligned with the one on the left. Although the Vestal who would soon take possession of this room probably wouldn't care, I could get a little obsessive-compulsive about things.

The Vestal Esmeralda…

The whole city was beside itself with excitement. Many Vestals had come through our temple, Our Lady of Paris, but she would be the first Anointed in over a century. And that made her a trophy Praetor Frollo would definitely want to add to his collection. But hopefully, he wouldn't tire of her as quickly as he had the others. The city's energy reserves were depleting quickly. As an Anointed, she would technically be able to summon far more power than the city had ever seen before and refill the Well.

The bedroom door opening startled me. I cursed myself inwardly for having allowed my mind to wander rather than properly triple check that nothing would meet his disapproval.

Frollo's tall and broad silhouette filled the door frame as his piercing blue eyes peered into the room with a severe gaze, assessing my work. My eyes flicked left and right, pleased with the stunning floral arrangements I had set around the room, before settling back on his sickeningly handsome face. He was the embodiment of perfection—everything I wasn't. Below-the-shoulder golden blond hair framed his rectangular face with a cleft chin. His wide mouth, with plush lips usually stretched in a suave smile when addressing the people, was currently pursed as he examined the room.

Despite his athletic physique, I was more muscular than he, and technically taller as well. But that wretched hump on my back systematically kept me in a bowed, servile position that gave off the impression he towered over me.

And I hated it.

Frollo lifted his straight, Roman nose at me, a satisfied expression on his face. "You've done well, Kwazeem," Frollo said in that deep voice that had the women in the city throw themselves at his feet. "This day needs to be perfect."

He walked around the room and ran a finger over the surface of the wide vanity before checking its tip for any traces of dust. I kept my hands behind my back to hide my fisting them in aggravation. The Praetor should know the cleaning staff was thorough when it came to a Vestal's quarters.

"Remember to remain out of sight when Esmeralda arrives," Frollo said in a stern voice, his gaze still searching the room for any flaw. "You are not to speak to her or come anywhere near her, even with your hood on. In fact, see that she remains oblivious of your presence. She is Anointed. Even the High Seraph is eager to make her acquaintance. But I am determined to make her mine."

I snorted inwardly. How could this foolish human possibly think he could rival an Elohim? The High Seraph Phoebus was pretty much a god in beauty, power, and charisma. Every single woman within the two planets and seven moons that formed the Nine Circles, be she Vestal or commoner, dreamed of becoming his consort.

Seeming fully satisfied at last, Frollo turned to look at me, his features taking on an almost paternal expression. This told me I was free at last. Although my face remained impassive, I internally breathed a heavy sigh of relief.

"Esmeralda's personal belongings are waiting in the Great Hall," the Praetor continued. "Would you be so kind as to bring them up, as well as the welcome basket Malina has prepared for my future mate? The staff is still scrambling to sort out the rest of the preparations, and I have more duties to attend before Esmeralda's arrival."

"Of course," I replied with a shrug. Although I wasn't a servant, I didn't mind performing these occasional tasks to help, especially as they gave me an excuse to traipse around areas of the temple I was normally forbidden access to.

"Thank you," Frollo said with genuine appreciation. "When you're done, go back to your quarters and remain there until I give you the all clear tomorrow. Your replicator should be full. You can have one of those meals for supper tonight and breakfast in the morning."

"Yes, Praetor," I said, hiding my disappointment. I had hoped to go hunt some game for my meal, rather than the lame leftovers I often received from the kitchen. But the replicator food was reasonably decent. "Will that be all?"

As soon as he nodded, I made a swift exit and headed for the lift. It was positioned in the middle of the back wall of the half-moon-shaped corridor. Four bedrooms occupied this floor, two on each side of the elevator. For Esmeralda, Frollo had conveniently chosen the bedroom adjacent to his, with a secret communicating door. The Praetor had done this in the past. However, there had usually been at least a couple more honorific guests conveniently occupying the other rooms.

But this was none of my concern.

The circular glass doors of the lift swished open before me, and the three rings of the round platform lit up when I stepped on it.

"Ground," I said, and the hovering platform swiftly flew down the ten stories of the temple's spire.

An eerie silence greeted me in the Great Hall. My steps echoed loudly in the large, empty room, with its tall, white columns covered with swirly patterns of light. I instinctively walked around the luminous symbol of Vesta etched with glow stones on the dark blue, polished stone floor that covered the hall. For some silly reason, walking over it always gave me the impression of trampling the goddess herself. Similar to the ancient Roman symbol on Earth, it was made out of two super-posed V shapes representing a brazier. However, the flame of old burning above it had been replaced by a glowing sun with electric sunrays.

To my surprise, Esmeralda had sent very little personal belongings. Only one ceremonial crate containing her Vestal dresses and two bags of luggage sat on the hovercart at the entrance of the hall.

I averted my eyes from the tall doors of the temple which opened onto the grand plaza and the Well of Power, which provided energy for the city and annexed towns. The doors had never opened for me. They never would. I was an abomination, a shameful secret that Frollo zealously protected... for my own safety.

Love and hatred filled my heart in equal measure as far as the Praetor was concerned. I lived by his mercy. He was my cold, indifferent 'jailor' and my only human contact. He had provided me with shelter, food, and protection. And once a month, he treated the terrible affliction that would otherwise either kill me or condemn me to a lifetime of agony. Even now, the dull pain at the base of my hump was steadily growing. By the time the Festival of Light came rolling in at the end of the week, it would reach excruciating levels that only the Praetor could relieve me of.

*And so I endure.*

With a sigh, I led the hovercart right beside the lift before going to fetch the welcome basket in the kitchen. Malina and the rest of the staff would be out on errands or other duties. Frollo would have never let me come down otherwise. The basket sat on a tray with two small covered dishes. The contents of the basket made my mouth water and my stomach rumble. Exotic fruits and cheeses, fresh breads, and a bottle of mulled wine enticed me. I didn't know what the two small plates contained but decided not to further torture myself by finding out.

When I got back to the tenth floor where Esmeralda's room was located, I was relieved to find her door open and Frollo gone.

As I finished laying down the tray on the table next to the large floor-to-ceiling window overlooking the plaza, I caught my reflection in the free-standing mirror on the opposite side of the room. I stared at myself with morbid fascination, my feet bringing me closer to it with a will of their own.

I would never pass for human with my bluish-grey skin, the scales on my shoulders and back, and the horns sitting on my forehead. But with my mysterious condition approaching its peak—usually over a thirty-day period—I was disfigured. My face and hands were heavily swollen. Large splotches had appeared beneath my skin, looking like huge, purplish bruises.

With the bloating, you would think I'd been on the losing end of a bloody fight. My only redeeming quality was my silver eyes. Even when my condition made them so puffy my eyelids were almost shut, they shone through, reminding me a worthy man lived behind that ugly mask. Soon, the Praetor would tend to my illness and, for a week or two, I'd be beautiful again.

I turned away from the mirror and neatly placed Esmeralda's luggage and ceremonial crate inside her large walk-in closet. After putting away the hovercart, I made my way to my room on the twelfth floor. Isolated from the rest of the world by the beacon which occupied the whole of the eleventh floor—formally called the Light of Vesta—the spire's summit was my haven and my window to the world.

To make sure no one would 'accidentally' stumble upon me, Frollo had cut down on the space in my room to add an antechamber outside the lift with a locked door to enter my quarters. I waved my hand in front of the bioscanner by the door, which slid open quietly. The happy chirps of my imps immediately greeted me, warming my heart. Victus and Lazarus flapped their grey batwings until they each landed on one of my shoulders. The claws of their tiny hands pricked my neck as they hugged me and carefully rubbed their faces on my cheeks.

"Hello, my friends," I said, gently pulling their long, pointy ears in my usual gesture of affection.

Victus chirped and climbed down the length of my arm to rest in the palm of my hand. Lifting his round, owlish face to gaze upon me, he gave me an expectant look until I started scratching the back of his ear. He squeaked with contentment, his tail wagging. Lazarus began braiding the right side of my shoulder length, midnight blue hair, a clear sign he'd been bored.

Walking past my king-sized bed—recently replaced to accommodate my tall frame—I headed for the kitchen area of my loft, which Frollo had furnished with high quality equipment, including a cooling unit, a replicator, and a cooking unit with an integrated grilling station. Unfortunately, my cooling unit stood empty, as Malina hadn't been able to get my groceries with all the frenzy surrounding the Vestal's arrival. Therefore, I selected a plate of boar meat with yam puree from my replicator. It wasn't fancy, but it would fill the hole in my belly.

I settled on the tall stool by the front window, overlooking the plaza. Often, I would sit here for hours, working on my wooden sculptures and looking at the people going about their daily lives. With windows on every wall but the back, there was always something worth watching in Paris. I couldn't be part of their world, but I made up dialogues and scenarios of what they were doing and saying. I invented a personality for most of them and named them accordingly.

But today, even as they scurried about, readying for the upcoming festival, the citizens of Paris failed to retain my attention. When my gaze didn't linger on Elysium—the distant floating city of the Elohim—it scanned the skies for the shuttle that would bring the Anointed. I ate distractedly, feeding tiny pieces of meat to my imps. They preferred it raw but, like me, they'd learned to be content with the comforts we had.

And then, just as the sun reached its zenith, its rays caught on the slick shape of a shuttle—a Light Chariot—descending towards the city. As one, the citizens and I all but froze, watching the pristine white vessel with the electric blue symbol of Vesta approach. It touched down on the landing pad located on the elevated plateau on the right side of the city.

Praetor Frollo, followed by an escort of six guards in ceremonial attire, and ten Light Maidens, took position at the foot of the stairs leading down from the landing pad. The guards, three on each side of the Praetor, held their lightning staves at arm's length, the bases resting on the ground, and the tips, sparkling with electric coils, pointing outwards. Pride swelled in my chest to have the weapons I'd created be used in this highly honorific setting.

The Maidens stood right in front of the staircase, five on each side. Their white, Grecian dress hid nothing of their sexy bodies. In truth, the dress was essentially a front and back panel of fabric held in place by three lumis cords: one beneath their breasts, the second at the waist, and the third directly beneath their buttocks, showing bare skin along their sides and hips. While pleasing to the eye, I felt no attraction towards them. Knowing they took turns warming Frollo's bed in the dumb hope he would take one of them as his consort was a major turn off.

But all thoughts of the Maidens faded when the tall and statuesque silhouette of Esmeralda stepped out of the shuttle. She paused at the top of the stairs leading down into the city. Despite the distance, my enhanced sight as a Fallen allowed me to see every detail of her astounding beauty, with her long and curly, reddish-brown hair, her oval face, and delicate, pointy nose. I couldn't tell if her sensual mouth with a plump bottom lip, or her sultry, green eyes mesmerized me the most. Under the bright, midday sun, her golden-brown skin—a delectable mix of hazelnut and cinnamon with a touch of honey—made my mouth water with the need to lick every inch of her.

With graceful movements, she delicately lifted the skirt of her traditional Vestal gown to climb down. If not for its expensive, shimmering white fabric, held at the shoulders by plaited lumis strings, the simple, virginal dress could have passed for a long, silk nightgown. Shoulders back, head straight, she descended the stairs with the regal presence of a queen.

Mindful of the lightning crackling at the tips of their staves, the crowd gathered in silence behind the guards. The Maidens spread their arms, palms up before them in an offering gesture. Electric coils rose from the skin along their arms, gathering into an orb in each of their hands. This should have been the extent of their greeting to the Vestal, but a beam of energy suddenly shot out of each orb forming an arc that connected with the beam from the orbs of the Maidens facing them. The crowd gasped at this display of power far beyond what the Maidens possessed. Their gaze shifted to the glowing archway the Maidens had created, which had been enabled by the powerful presence of the Anointed.

Even from where I stood, high up in the spire and so far away from the Vestal, I could feel the power swirling within her like a caged beast hungry to be set free. And it stirred something deep within me that I didn't understand, but that I instinctively knew had been lying dormant, waiting to be awakened.

Waiting for her.

Esmeralda nodded at each of the Maidens in greeting as she passed under their glowing archway at the end of which Frollo was waiting for her. Anger blossomed within me at the appreciative glance she cast at the Praetor while exchanging greetings with him. When he took her hand and lifted it to his lips to kiss her knuckles, my anger turned into a seething rage. My imps, Victus and Lazarus, chirping with concern made me realize I was emitting an animalistic growl. I quieted down and noticed that my claws had come out and scratched the surface of the wooden shelf I'd been using as both a dining and working table.

Averting my eyes, I tried to rein in the irrational, possessive fury that the sight of a female I didn't even know had instilled in me. The Praetor had warned me to stay away from the Vestals. Apparently, Fallen like me could corrupt their purity and sever their link to Vesta. I had always refused to believe that mere genetics could push people into doing terrible things. Over the years, I'd seen many Vestals that left me mostly indifferent. But this Anointed, the breathtaking Esmeralda, I wanted to claim, to possess, and to defile in every possible way.

# CHAPTER 2
## ESMERALDA

Only years of training and preparing for this moment kept me from running back into the shuttle in a fit of panic. I had dreamed of the day the citizens of one of the moons of the Nine Circles would greet me with enthusiasm as I brought them the light and power of Vesta. But even in the wildest of those dreams, I had never dared to hope it would be with such grandeur, and least of all in Paris—the capital city of the seat of the Elohim.

As the Chariot of Light had flown over the city, I'd been blown away by the sheer size of its Well of Power in the center of the plaza. It made sense it would be so massive considering the sprawling city would require a lot of energy, not to mention the surrounding suburbs. Despite being confident in my power, I had never charged a Well of this magnitude. Knowing my first time doing so would be during the Festival of Light, the greatest annual event in the Nine Circles, had me anxious. That it would also be in the presence of Phoebus, the High Seraph of the First Circle, made me feel faint.

Coming down the stairs into the city with so many eyes on me had been extremely intimidating. Thankfully, the weak power of the Maidens had given me something to focus on. As my power seeped into them to form the energy arches, the people's awe did wonders in boosting my confidence. If so little sufficed to impress them, then maybe… just maybe, I wouldn't fare too poorly here.

As a newly ordained Vestal, my initial assignment should have been on one of the seven moons of the Nine Circles. Normally, it would have been between the Seventh and the Ninth Circle. Considering my greater power, I had expected to land on one of the moons named Fourth to Sixth Circle. However, being Anointed, a Vestal with off the charts powers whether through Chanting or dancing, meant I would begin directly on one of the two planets around which those moons orbited. The planet Zion—also known as the Second Circle, would have been a tremendous honor. But Praetor Frollo had personally sent me a formal invitation to the capital city of planet Eden, the First Circle.

And he was magnificent.

Many had speculated that the grand administrator of the most powerful city of the First Circle had angelic DNA. Born of a humble family, he had steadily climbed the ranks of the magistrates until fifteen years ago. A few months after reaching his majority, his energy manipulation abilities had suddenly skyrocketed—a common trait in Archangels and Seraphs. In light of his tremendous power, he had, unsurprisingly, become the youngest Praetor of Paris, or of any of the Circles for that matter. Even as I stood before him, I could feel the supernatural power emanating from him; power that I could only assume to be angelic as I had yet to be directly in the presence of an Elohim.

But that alien power awakened something inside me that I had never felt before. Something that stirred and enhanced my own. However, I had expected it to hum more strongly within him, like a great aura that sizzled around him and that would draw me like a magnet. Maybe it merely lay dormant since he currently wasn't using it.

Still, my skin tingled when he pressed his lips to the back of my hand in greeting. I almost felt sorry when he let go.

"Greeting, Blessed Esmeralda, and welcome to Paris. We are honored by the presence of an Anointed in our midst," the Praetor said in his rather pleasant, deep, suave voice, while pressing a palm to his heart.

I suspected that, beyond courtesy, the gesture had meant to draw my attention to his body, and the skin-tight white shirt that hid nothing of the deep grooves of his chiseled abs, with the lumis embroidery emphasizing every curve of his muscular chest and narrow waist. His subtle flirting flattered me, but I was in no hurry. It was common for Vestals to bed or marry their Praetor. However, my focus for now remained on the upcoming Festival… and meeting High Seraph Phoebus.

"The honor is all mine, Praetor Frollo," I said with sincerity. "But please, no titles required. I am not very formal. You may simply call me Esmeralda or Mera, as most of my friends do."

"Then, *Mera*, I must insist you call me Frollo," he said with a beaming smile. I nodded in response, and he gestured towards the temple. "Come, you must be tired after such a long trip. Here is Our Lady of Paris, your new home. I hope it will live up to your expectations."

"I'm sure it will exceed them," I said with a grateful smile.

It had indeed been a long trip from the dark moon Obscura, the Fifth Circle where the Temple of Vesta was erected. I had spent the past nineteen years of my life there, being trained since the age of six to serve the Citizens of the Light.

Moving past the stalls of the open market on each side of the plaza, we walked over the reinforced glass pane which covered the Well of Power currently recessed into the ground. The slow, pulsating glow of the markings on the Well intensified as I strolled over it. I welcomed the gentle caress of its energy poking at me.

"The Well approves of you," Frollo said, with a seductive smile.

"And I of it," I replied, playing along, although the Well wasn't a sentient being.

As we strolled towards the temple, I let my gaze roam over its beautiful white columns, the ornate frescos around the top edges of the walls, the statues of the different orders of angels, but mainly of Seraphs with their lightning staves, lances, and bows, and the tall spire in the center. It rose like a giant sword stabbing at the heart of Our Lady of Paris. The pommel constituted the beacon, the Light of Vesta, which represented life, hope, health, and prosperity for our people: our light into the darkness. In practice, however, it merely meant power flowed through the realm. Directly connected to the Well, a single beam of light ran up the 'sword' to the beacon that shone bright for the whole realm to see. Woe unto anyone who allowed it to go out.

But even as Frollo casually told me of the accommodations he had prepared for me and of the temple's schedule, my eyes kept being drawn to the beacon. I couldn't say why, but something was calling out to me. Forcing myself to pay attention to the Praetor, I averted my eyes confused by the pull that only grew the closer we came to Our Lady of Paris.

After we climbed the steps to the massive doors of the temple, Vesta's symbol carved on them lit up, and then they parted before us. The guards lined up on each side of the doors let us through. They remained outside while the Maidens followed in behind us.

The greeting hall was everything I had expected, with the luminous, intricate carvings on the walls, and more pillars. Wall sconces shaped like ornate braziers, with a hovering orb of energy instead of flames, lit the room. Tall windows let the rays of the midday sun flood in. At the back, on each side of the circular lift, two doorways gave access to what I assumed would be the chapel. Sideways-facing Seraph statues carved into the doorframe gave the impression they were holding the top of the frame.

We stopped in front of the elevator and, after a respectful bow of their heads, the Maidens filed into the room beyond, four on each side. I'd be joining them later for the evening Chant and to prepare for the Chakra services in the morning.

"Let me show you to your suite," Frollo said, waving a hand towards the elevator.

"Thank you," I replied with gratitude.

His palm settling on the small of my back to give me a slight nudge forward startled me. You didn't touch a Vestal without her express consent. His kissing the back of my hand earlier had been inappropriate. But in public, it could be deemed innocent. With the two of us alone, it spoke of a bit too much familiarity that I would need to keep in check. Not wanting to make a scene so soon after my arrival, I let it slide, especially considering his touch had been brief—and not actually unpleasant. However, I needed to carefully manage his expectations and mine.

As we reached the tenth floor, I swiftly stepped out of the lift just as his hand started moving towards my back again, avoiding his touch. The discreet smile on his lips told me he wasn't fooled. That suited me perfectly. The message had been conveyed without needing to be spelled out... I hoped.

We walked past the first door to the left of the elevator to another door on the side wall. My jaw dropped at the opulence of the room beyond. The massive room was bigger than the dorm I had shared with twenty other Initiates upon my arrival on Obscura, and for my first ten years there. Besides the imposing bed, big enough for four adults, the room had its own en suite with a full bathroom, walk-in closet, a music area, work area, breakfast table, and sitting area. Many large windows gave a breathtaking view of the east side of Paris, with the other set of windows overlooking the plaza.

"This is stunning," I said to Frollo, who had followed me inside the room. "You certainly know how to make your guests feel welcomed."

"You are not just a guest, Mera," he said, his voice dipping into baritone. "This is your home now. Maybe your permanent home…"

"Still very welcoming of you," I said, pretending not to understand his underlying meaning.

It was both flattering and slightly irritating. I didn't like a man coming on too strong, and he'd been right about the trip having been tiring. Finding him a little too close for comfort, I walked towards the table where a tray laden with appetizing food waiting to be devoured sat.

"Very thoughtful of you," I said, waving at the food. "I hadn't realized how famished I was, until now. A shower, a quick meal, and a short nap should have me in top shape for tonight's Chant."

Once again, his smirk conveyed that he wasn't fooled. "I will let you rest then. If you need anything, my room is just next door."

My smile stiffened on my face, but I nonetheless managed to nod graciously. "I doubt that will be the case, but thank you."

Frollo pressed his palm to his chest as he had done earlier, bowed his head, and then left my quarters. I closed and locked the door behind him, feeling somehow violated. I didn't understand my strongly negative reaction to his open flirtation. After all, I had come here in the hopes of marrying him should none of the Elohim wish to take me as his consort. A Vestal couldn't hope for a better prospect than the Praetor of Paris. He was drop dead gorgeous, and it was common practice for a Praetor to pop a Vestal's cherry.

Technically, we weren't forbidden to have sex to serve Vesta, but the choices were pretty slim and mostly unappealing on Obscura. In fact, I always suspected it was intentional so that we would save ourselves for the Elohim. Many of the Vestals counted the days until they could finally get down and dirty. To be honest, so had I. And I still did. Which made my reaction all the more bizarre. I should be honored he would make his interest known. The contrary would have probably offended me. And yet, that we should share neighboring bedrooms felt presumptuous of him, if not disrespectful. While his energy drew me like a magnet, something about him turned me off. Even now, I could feel his divine aura all around the room. The temple was suffused with it.

Shaking the confusing thoughts, I settled at the table and gorged on the food before taking a quick shower. I never took that nap, unpacking my belongings instead and meditating to realign my chakras. Tonight's Chant would be the first test. Frollo hadn't requested my presence a week before the Festival so that I could enjoy an extended vacation, but to see if I could charge his city. If I failed to demonstrate my power over the next few days, I would be sent back to Obscura in shame.

And *that* was not an option.

# CHAPTER 3
### KWAZEEM

I paced my room with increasing agitation, further fueled by my imps chirping and flying around me. I wanted to go down to the chapel to listen to the Chant, and to steal a close up view of Esmeralda. If I hid on the balcony, no one would be the wiser. I didn't even have to take the elevator. The temple had many hidden passages that no one used anymore; all of which I was intimately familiar with.

Although they couldn't speak with words, the imps were highly intelligent. Over the years, we had developed our own sign language through which they could communicate their thoughts to me. Victus glared at me and signed for me to go. Both he and Lazarus hated that I remained locked away in my room while life passed me by. No matter how many times I'd explained to them that I might get killed or chased out of town if the citizens knew a Fallen hybrid lived in their midst, they persisted I should go out into the world.

But this… This I could indulge in and get away with. Even now, I could feel her power swirling around me, beckoning me.

"Okay. Okay, I will go," I said to them, although it was more to convince myself I would truly do this.

The imps chirped their happiness, hugged my neck, and gave me a kiss before flying towards an inconspicuous section of the wall. I waved my hand in a specific pattern before the hidden motion detector. The wall panel opened revealing a secret passage to the emergency staircase. I made my way down the stairs… the endless flights of stairs.

It was no problem at first, but halfway through the ten stories I had to climb down, each step I took resonated painfully in the middle of my spine. It was there that the wretched fluid that tortured and disfigured me accumulated at the base of my hump over a month's period. In five days, Frollo would drain it out for me, relieving me of my suffering. And for a week or two after that, the swelling and the blotching would go away. If not for the hump, I would look normal… handsome even.

But I was committed. No pain would keep me from my prize and the powerful lure of the Vestal's enticing energy. Dim at first, the sound of an angelic voice gradually grew as I approached my destination. Victus squealed with excitement.

"Hush!" I hissed in a low voice. "You will give us away!"

Hovering next to me, Victus covered his mouth with both hands and gave me a sheepish look with his big, beady black eyes. He was so adorable, I couldn't be angry with him, even if I'd wanted to. I tapped my left shoulder, indicating I wasn't mad, and he eagerly landed on it before cuddling against my neck. Not wanting to be left out, Lazarus settled on my right shoulder and imitated his brother. I smiled and finished my descent along the rest of the stairs to the second floor, clenching my teeth through the pain.

I opened another secret panel which revealed a hidden staircase that stopped halfway between the second floor and the ground floor. A dark passage led to the balcony of the chapel. A regular human would have needed some kind of light to see, but thanks to my Fallen heritage, I had perfect night vision. Trying to ignore the divine sound of Esmeralda's voice, I pressed my ear to the panel that would part to grant me access to the balcony and listened for any movement on the other side.

Not hearing or sensing any presence, I silently slid it open. A wave of power slammed into me, and I almost whimpered as my knees wobbled beneath me. The crystalline sound of her voice penetrated deep within me and into my very soul. I snuck onto the balcony on shaky legs, mesmerized by her Chant. But with each note, a strange energy pulsated in my chest. As it grew, so did the stabbing pain in my back. I ignored it, advancing in a half-crouch in front of the empty benches to look through the ornate bars of the ramp at the dais inside the chapel.

Barefoot, clad in a traditional ceremonial Roman dress, the white fabric tightly cinched at her narrow waist, Esmeralda looked like an innocent young nymph. Hands held before her, palms up in a gesture of devotion, she sang in the old tongue, facing the altar of Vesta—which was essentially an energy collector. Behind her, the Maidens each held Light Orbs, which they attempted to attune to Esmeralda's energy signature. They obviously didn't have her power level, but like leeches, once properly aligned with her, they would feed off the Vestal's energy to manipulate to their own will.

And behind the Maidens, sitting by himself on one of the ground floor benches, Frollo stared at Esmeralda with a hungry, predatory look that made my blood boil, my fangs descend, and my claws stick out. I knew that look well, but he wouldn't have her.

Not her. Not ever.

But even as I burned with possessive anger, my skin began to crackle with energy. Tendrils of electricity appeared along my arms, writhing and coiling with accrued strength around my hands. I stared in fascination at the phenomenon, feeling an incredible surge of energy within me. At the same time, Esmeralda's voice became louder, richer, fuller. Similar electric tendrils to those covering me began to form over her extended arms and around the altar.

As Frollo rose to his feet, mouth gaping at Esmeralda's incredible display of power, I fell to my knees, teeth clenched in pain. The Chant filled me with something akin to physical pleasure—almost orgasmic in its nature—and a tremendous sense of power. At the same time, pure agony coursed through me as the Chant intensified the symptoms of my condition. My face throbbed and was swelling at an exponential rate. My skin felt on the verge of splitting open, and ghostly hands were frantically stabbing at my hump with a searing hot blade.

By the time I broke free of the trance the Chant had put me under, I could barely refrain from crying out in agony. My vision blurred and my stomach roiled as I attempted to crawl on all fours towards the hidden passage. I didn't even cross a meter before I collapsed. A strangled cry rose from my throat while my imps flew around my head in panic.

The Chant abruptly stopped. The only sound echoing through the room was the muffled thump of my convulsing limbs. Victus flew over the railing to seek out Frollo for help. The Maidens gasped and squealed in fear, while Esmeralda merely gaped in shock. Victus signed to Frollo to come rescue me. The Praetor obviously didn't understand the message, but the fury contorting his features revealed he at least understood that I had disobeyed his order to stay in my quarters.

The excruciating pain torturing me overrode the worry that would normally seize me at the prospect of his justified wrath. Right now, I just wished to lose consciousness so that I no longer felt like my spine was being repeatedly torn right out of my back. But I was trapped in this endless well of misery.

"You little vermin," Frollo hissed.

Raising his palm towards Victus, Frollo sent out a bolt of lightning, hitting the imp square in the chest. I shouted for him to stop, but only a tortured groan got past my lips. Victus flopped to the floor, stunned. Lazarus squeaked in fear while his brother weakly flapped his wings.

"NO!" Esmeralda shouted when Frollo made to zap the imp again. She rushed down from the dais to pick up Victus.

"This creature shouldn't be inside this sacred temple," Frollo said in a hard voice. "I've been too soft with my gardener. Apologies that such a powerful Chant should have been so rudely interrupted."

"It's okay," Esmeralda said, looking disturbed by Frollo's anger. "I believe we are sufficiently attuned, anyway." She cast a look towards the Maidens seeking confirmation. They all nodded while staring warily at the imp.

Victus, flapping his wings again, flew drunkenly out of Esmeralda's grasp and towards me.

"I think there's someone up there," Esmeralda said, her voice filled with concern. "Someone in pain. Could it be your gardener?"

"Do not worry. I will handle it," Frollo said in a clipped tone. "You've had a long day, and a longer one still awaits you in the morning. I will see you tomorrow.

Esmeralda hesitated, casting a worried glance up at the balcony before caving. She exited the room, and instead of hastening to my side, Frollo stared at the balcony with murder in his eyes. My own eyes felt like they were being squished inside my skull. Despite his dizziness, Victus poured what little healing abilities he possessed into me to try and lessen my pain, imitated by his brother. But I was beyond their assistance.

The electric coils that had danced over my skin and the intense power I'd felt within faded with Esmeralda's departure. I was left with nothing but the abysmal torment from which the Praetor didn't seem too eager to relieve me. Pained moans poured out of me in a steady stream for an eternity. I didn't know if I'd lost consciousness, but Frollo's hand suddenly yanking me onto a hover stretcher sent a new wave of agony through my body, and this time, blessed darkness fell before my eyes.

I came to lying on my stomach on the hover stretcher. The familiar disinfectant scent of Frollo's lab filled my nose. Despite the atrocious pain that continued to rack my body, I could have wept with anticipatory joy, knowing that soon, very soon, it would be taken away.

"I should leave you like this," Frollo hissed, noisily preparing his tools for the procedure. "I should leave you like this through the night to teach you not to disobey me. What the fuck were you thinking?" he shouted, standing before me, his hand fisting the spinal tap needle as if he wanted to stab me with it. "Do you have a death wish?"

I tried to shake my head, but my body barely responded.

"I asked you a fucking question!" Frollo yelled, making my ears ring.

"N… n… no," I barely managed to answer.

"Have I not told you time and time again what the Citizens would do to a Fallen if they discovered you? And you brought your wretched imps with you. The Maidens and the Anointed have seen the vermin. Imps only become familiars to Fallen."

Frollo yanked up my shirt over my back in a brutal motion that sent stabbing pain along my spine and down my legs. I cried out and, eyes rolling in my head, I fought to remain conscious.

"Fifteen years I've devoted to protecting your sorry ass, and this is how you repay me? It's one thing to put your life at risk for a pretty Vestal, but you're okay putting mine on the line as well?"

Frollo didn't wait for an answer that I wouldn't have been able to voice anyway. Using no anesthesia and showing none of his usual care for my discomfort, the Praetor jabbed the needle at the base of my hump along my spine. I thought my face would split from my mouth opening too wide to roar with agony. For a few seconds, the pain further increased—not that I would have thought it possible—and then pure bliss as the pressure faded from my back.

"You will no longer stay in the temple," Frollo said in a cold voice, removing the full tube of glowing, silver liquid drained from my back, to attach a new one to the needle. "The construction of your cabin is advanced enough to be habitable now. Leave tonight when everyone is asleep. Tomorrow, I'll have my personal guards bring you the rest of your heavier belongings. See that you remain out of sight."

My heart ached at losing my room at the very top of the spire. It had been my window on the world, giving me the illusion that, somehow, I belonged. Located in a remote corner of the temple's garden, hidden from view by trees and bushes, my cabin was shaping up to be a beautiful home. I had built it myself in my spare time. It was close to the river where I often fished, and near the woods where I occasionally hunted game. Although it would make a lovely home, it would also isolate me more than ever; out of sight and out of mind.

And worse still, it would keep me away from my wo… from Esmeralda.

"I'm sorry, Praetor," I said in a weak, broken voice. "I had only wanted to listen to the Chant."

"You could have listened on the day of the Festival, from the safety of your balcony," Frollo snapped. "Now, you have even lost that! See that you do not lose more."

I opened my mouth to argue, but he cut me off with a series of questions about my condition. Normally, after thirty days, he only drained two and a half vials of silver liquid from my hump. But right now, he had already drawn four vials, and was working on a fifth. I didn't know why it had escalated so fast and so soon; only that the Vestal's presence—and especially her voice—had stirred some kind of energy within me that spurred on my illness.

A troubled look crossed Frollo's face as he studied mine. It no longer ached or felt stretched to the point of bursting anymore. In a couple of hours from now, I would look hand-some. To my shame, that thought immediately conjured up a scene where Esmeralda would get to see my face and find me more attractive than the Praetor.

As if he'd guessed the nature of my thoughts, Frollo's face took on an angry edge, and he gave me a hard stare. Finished at last, he placed the fifth vial—two-thirds full—on the tray by the hover stretcher I'd been lying on.

"We're done here. Go back to your quarters, and do not use the lift," Frollo said with contempt. "You've exposed yourself enough for one day. Remember, be gone tonight and stay the fuck away from Mera. I intend to make her my wife, and I will not have her scared off by you."

*Mera.*

The familiarity with which he used her nickname triggered a rabid anger inside me. I fisted my hands to prevent my claws from shooting out and shredding his pretty face to pieces. I didn't know why I felt so possessive of her. Granted, she was stunningly beautiful, but Frollo only ever invited attractive Vestals to Paris. None of the previous ones had stirred me like Esmeralda did. I bit my tongue so as not to tell him that he could never have what was mine.

The Praetor gestured with his head for me to get off the stretcher. Obedient, I complied, my entire body still aching from the violent spasms that had racked it earlier.

"Thank you for helping me," I said, standing on unsteady feet.

The words scorched my tongue. Although I genuinely was grateful to be free of the pain, he hadn't done it out of compas-sion or love for me. I was a useful tool and 'free' labor that he exploited in exchange for his 'protection' against those who would harm me. But now that I was banished from the temple, did it even make sense for me to stay here, choking under his tight leash? If I were to be isolated, I could be isolated and free in the wilderness of the First Circle.

*But then you would never see Esmeralda again.*

Frollo harrumphed his acknowledgment of my gratitude, then headed to the wall panel that he opened onto the hidden passage. The lab and his quarters were the only rooms to which the bioscanners would not grant me access. With heavy steps, I padded towards the doorway and into the staircase passage.

"And, Kwazeem," Frollo called out behind me, "I can only drain you so many times before your spine sustains permanent damage. Disobey me again, and the next time, I will let you enjoy the pain for an entire day… or two."

Hands fisted before me so he wouldn't see them, I looked at the Praetor over my shoulder, forcing a repentant expression on my face. "Understood, Praetor."

Without another word, Frollo closed the secret door in my face. Silencing the resentment in my heart, I focused my energy on climbing the nine stories from the third floor where the lab was located to my room on the twelfth. My muscles screamed in protest, but I ignored them, too.

Nothing, and no one, would break me—least of all, pain.

# CHAPTER 4
## ESMERALDA

After draping my white sarong into a one-shoulder dress, I slipped on a pair of flat sandals and quickly brushed my long, curly hair. For a moment, I considered tying it up but decided to let it flow freely down my back.

The thought of breakfast with Frollo had lost its appeal last night. Him zapping the imp, clearly in distress and coming to him for assistance, had been shocking. That he'd intended to actually kill it had been repulsive. Granted, imps were not naturally welcomed among the human colonies of the Nine Circles. While mostly non-aggressive, they usually sought the companionship of Fallen the same way dogs sought that of humans. So, what in the world was it doing in Vesta's temple of all places?

But the indifferent way in which he had reacted to his gardener's malaise had truly disturbed me. While I didn't approve of cruelty towards pets, that he'd been so laid-back about another human being's suffering spoke volumes about his questionable morals and apparent lack of empathy. Even if the Attunement Chant was meant to be a private affair, there had been no harm in the gardener sneaking in quietly to listen.

Punishing him for this inoffensive indiscretion felt disproportionately cruel.

I had almost gone up to the balcony myself to tend to the man—or at least, I assumed it had been a man. However, I'd gotten the strong feeling Frollo simply wanted me gone so that he could do so away from prying eyes. It raised a billion questions in my mind as to why he would want to hide his gardener from us.

Sighing heavily, I took a final glance at my reflection in the mirror. I frowned at the absence of earrings dangling from my earlobes. Where many women felt naked without makeup on, for me, it was earrings. I hesitated, not wanting to 'pretty' myself up too much so that Frollo wouldn't think it was all for him, then immediately chastised myself for the thought. I wouldn't let his unfounded wishes and expectations dictate how I dressed or went about my life. Thankfully, unlike many of the ceremonial dresses, my personal outfits were more on the demure side, enough not to be perceived as an invitation. After putting on a pair of silver earrings with a large emerald stone matching my eyes, I stopped dallying and made my way down to the second floor of the spire.

The minute the dining room doors opened, the potent wave of energy that struck me nearly made my knees buckle. Male, raw, divine, it coursed through me like the most powerful of aphrodisiacs. And the source of this irresistible power? Frollo.

Standing with his back to me, looking through the large window at the plaza below, he seemed taller, broader, his muscles even more defined than in my memory. No doubt sensing my presence, he turned around to face me, and my breath caught in my throat. With the sun bathing his golden mane and pristine second skin of a shirt with its early morning rays, the Praetor appeared to glow with an angelic halo.

My feet irresistibly carried me towards him. With an elegant, almost feline gait, my host met me halfway. I felt dizzy, intoxicated by his presence. My nipples hardened, and moisture pooled between my thighs as he stopped two steps in front of me, his male scent acting like a potent pheromone.

I didn't understand what was happening to me. All my misgivings about him, all the disdain he had elicited in me had evaporated. If he were to take me to his bedroom this instant, I would follow him gladly. Heck, if he tossed me on top of the table right now and ravished me, I would not only welcome it, I'd spur him on.

Frollo extended a hand towards me, which I instinctively took. Lightning literally struck, electric tendrils swirling over our hands and skin when they touched. I gasped, my mouth parting in shock. A triumphant smile stretched his sensual lips. It should have upset me, but my stomach flip-flopped instead with desire. His blue eyes darkened as they lowered to stare at my lips. Mouth dry, my pulse increased as I waited with burning anticipation for him to kiss me.

Just as he leaned forward, the kitchen door opened with two servants bringing out our food. I instinctively yanked my hand out of his grasp, my cheeks heating like a teen caught red-handed. Frollo clenched his jaw and pinched his lips. The hard glimmer in his eyes as he watched the servants approach doused the insane arousal that had robbed me of my sanity.

With his palm pressed against the small of my back, Frollo led me to that imposing dining table. Midnight blue, with a single, pale blue, luminous line near each edge on the longer side, it contrasted sharply with the mostly white or pale colors of the room. Minimalist in its design, the rectangular room was simply adorned with a glowing symbol of Vesta on the left wall, with life-size statues of Vestals on each side of it. On the opposite side, framing the door into the kitchen, two Seraph statues held their swords before them with both hands, the tips resting on the ground.

We settled at the dining table with me facing the window and

Frollo sitting across from me. I didn't know if it had been intentional so that the sun continued to give him that angelic halo, but I was grateful regardless. Although he continued to affect me in an irrational fashion, a bit of distance allowed me to collect my thoughts. This powerful aura surrounding the Praetor, the potent energy bubbling within him like a volcano on the verge of erupting, and his irresistible—almost charismatic—appeal were all the things I had expected to feel the first time we had met outside the landing pad.

And yet, something didn't quite add up. His energy spoke to mine, lifted it up and made it stronger. I had felt it last night during the Chant. Even as an Anointed, I'd never felt so powerful. But I could have sworn it hadn't come from him. I'd been too focused on the song and on helping the Maidens attune to me to notice it at first. And then, a steady surge of energy had flowed through me. I'd felt invincible, like a goddess even.

Thinking back on it now, it had almost felt like a spiritual connection to something greater, magical... to whomever had been on the balcony.

That made no sense.

And right now, I could clearly see—feel—that Frollo had been the one enhancing me. Only a soulmate could create that kind of connection. I gazed upon the Praetor's handsome face with new eyes. He was everything a woman could want. So why, even with the potent attraction that kept making me want to jump over the table to have my way with him, did this sense of unease continue to plague me?

We remained silent while the servants filled our plates with a hearty breakfast of cold and hot meats, cheeses, hot breads, fresh fruits, steamed vegetables and sautéed potatoes. It wasn't uncommon on the Nine Circles planets and moons for breakfast to be the main course of the day, with two lighter meals afterwards: lunch in late afternoon and dinner at sundown.

"You look even more radiant this morning," Frollo said with a purring voice, the minute the servants left the room.

"Thank you," I said after taking a large sip of black coffee to help me regain control of my jumbled thoughts and emotions. "How could I not after such a wonderful night's sleep in a bed fit for a queen?"

It had not been the answer he'd hoped for. The glint of displeasure in his eyes further helped me disperse the haze that was robbing me of common sense.

"I'm glad you are enjoying the accommodations," Frollo replied, being a surprisingly good sport, considering just moments ago, I'd have let him take my virginity right on the stone floor of the dining room. And he knew it, too. "Maybe Paris… and its people… will seduce you enough to make it a permanent stay."

"Time will tell," I said, in a non-committal tone, while buttering a warm piece of whole wheat baguette. "But then, maybe the citizens of Paris will send me packing after the Festival," I said teasingly, steering the conversation onto a safer topic.

Frollo snorted as if I'd said something silly. "In light of the tremendous power you displayed last night, the citizens of Paris will do absolutely everything humanly possible to keep you. *Everything*," he reiterated, his underlying meaning crystal clear. "The city has greatly expanded over the past few years. None of the previous Vestals have been powerful enough to fully recharge the Well because too many dwellings and surrounding rural cities depend on it. With what you've done during the Chant, you will have everyone on their knees in awe during the Festival."

I hadn't been fishing for compliments, but I couldn't deny his words both flattered me and alleviated some of my nerves.

"I don't know about that," I said shyly, "but I have high hopes that my efforts will significantly help the city's reserves."

"They will," Frollo replied with confidence, after washing down his meal with a sip of coffee. "However, filling the Well is only one part of the ceremony. You will also have five Relay Orbs to charge at the same time. Do not worry," he added quickly at my flabbergasted expression. "We do not expect you to be able to fill such a huge Well *and* five Relay Orbs. As soon as the Well of Power is halfway full, all the extra energy you generate will be transferred to the Relays until they are full. And if, by the grace of Vesta, you still have more to offer, then the rest will go back to the Well."

I nodded, only partially relieved. Still, half of such a massive well was no small task.

"Do not worry so much," Frollo said in a sympathetic tone. "As per standard practice for Paris, there are always two more Vestals in attendance to provide additional support if needed. But you certainly won't."

"Your trust flatters me," I said with sincerity.

"I had high faith before you even arrived, based on your score from Obscura. But now that I saw you in action last night, I have no fear," Frollo said, matter-of-factly. "Be aware that, after the ceremony, you, the High Seraph, and I will take part in a banquet on the grand plaza with the people. Afterwards, I will fly with the Relay Orbs to each of the five main cities surrounding Paris and will not return until late the next day. Should you not choose to remain in the capital city with the Elohim, I would be honored if you chose to travel with me instead."

My stomach dropped. There it was, all the cards on the table. If one of the Elohim didn't court me, or if I didn't choose to favorably answer any advance they might make to me, the Praetor hoped I would go with him as his consort. You didn't take a lover on official trips, only a spouse. Despite my continued attraction towards him because of that insanely seductive aura of his, that prospect made me uneasy. It shouldn't have. I'd first feared he only wanted to add me to his list of conquests, but that was clearly not the case.

"You greatly honor me, Frollo. I will be sure to let you know of my decision before the end of the Festival," I said with a gentle smile.

To my relief, he graciously accepted my non-committal answer and steered the conversation onto more mundane discussions about life in Paris and the complexity of managing a city this size with so many dependent peripheral towns. Our meal ended in a relaxed atmosphere. Still, a wave of relief washed over me when the Praetor took his leave to go tend to his many duties as magistrate of the city.

Confused by the contradicting emotions and physical responses my host stirred within me, I decided to take a walk through the garden at the back of the temple. I wasn't in the mood to traipse through the streets of Paris, always crowded, with countless eyes that would inevitably stare at me like an odd insect. I needed some peace and quiet to clear my thoughts.

The garden was magnificent, with an exquisite selection of colorful plants, plush bushes with long leaves, and tall trees with droopy branches covered with pale or white flowers. Everything was flawlessly maintained and trimmed. I stopped by a large pond where a few duck-like birds I didn't recognize were swimming leisurely. Closing my eyes, I spread my arms wide and focused on the soft chirping of the birds in the nearby trees and the gentle rustling of the wind in the leaves.

As peace descended over me, tension draining from my shoulders, an odd chirping to my right broke through the harmonious whistling of the birds. My eyes popped open, and my head jerked to the right only to find myself face to face with the imp from last night, hovering in place at my eye level.

It bared its sharp, tiny teeth at me. I instinctively recoiled before it dawned on me it was probably a smile. The creature hid its teeth, his previously engaging demeanor becoming wary.

"It's okay, little one," I said in a soft voice, extending a hand towards it. "You just startled me. I'm not going to hurt you."

All tension left its small shoulders, and it flew towards my hand, landing carefully in the middle of my palm. I lifted it close to my face to look into its beady eyes, shining like two enormous black pearls. Reaching with its little hands, the imp grabbed my cheek, its claws slightly pricking my skin without hurting or piercing it. Drawing my face towards its own, the imp gave my chin a gentle kiss, before letting me go with a sheepish look on its adorable little owlish face.

"You probably shouldn't be lurking around here," I said with a gentle voice, caressing the tip of his pointy ear with my index finger. "I don't want the Praetor hurting you again."

The imp scrunched its face in displeasure at hearing the mention of Frollo. Its small hands moved quickly in a series of gestures I assumed to be some kind of sign language.

"I don't understand," I said, apologetically.

The creature scrunched its face again with a look that implied I had failed it, which made me laugh. Flapping its wings, the imp flew away a few meters, stopped to look at me over its shoulder, and waved for me to follow. My head told me I probably shouldn't, but my gut told me to proceed.

The imp didn't rush me, coming back to circle around me while I made my way in the general direction he was leading me. We crossed the entire garden, and as we approached a dead-end of thick bushes, decorative rocks, and colorful flowers tastefully landscaped, my steps faltered in confusion. But the imp continued forward before making a hard left turn, disappearing behind the wall of foliage.

My jaw dropped, realizing that the clever arrangement had created an optical illusion dissimulating a path further hidden by a curtain of vines. I brushed them aside, blown away by the neatly kept winding pathway leading farther away from the temple.

As I cleared a tall, neatly trimmed hedge, the silhouette of a humble, but solidly built house appeared in my line of sight.

Even before seeing him, I knew the imp had lured me to the gardener. Unconsciously, I had known where the creature was taking me the instant he'd gestured for me to follow.

But instead of the wizened older man, maybe reformed old convict I had expected to see, a true god stood before me. At least seven feet tall, muscles for days on his massive arms and chiseled abs, with the angelic face of a Seraph, he was single handedly lifting a beam that would have normally required the effort of half a dozen human men.

His head suddenly jerked towards me, and his mesmerizing silver eyes widened, hypnotizing me. The pull, the connection I had felt in the chapel last night immediately formed again. And yet, it was weaker, dimmed somehow. The beam dropping to the ground with a loud thump snapped me out of my frozen state.

Only then did the greyish-blue tinge of his skin, the thick scales on his neck and shoulders, and the horns on his forehead finally register. He was a Fallen, not an Elohim.

# CHAPTER 5
## KWAZEEM

I sensed her presence moments before Victus came flying around my head, chirping proudly to have lured my woman to me. The fool. The mere sight of her instantly set my blood to boiling and had my stomach contracting painfully with desire. Of all the reactions Esmeralda could have had upon seeing me, I never would have expected the look of awe and wonder in her eyes that seemed to undress me. It only further fanned the flame that had ignited within me. In the last fifteen years of my twenty-eight years of existence, I had only ever known pity, anger, or indifference.

The bond I systematically felt in her presence formed again, and her tremendous power awakened a strange one inside of me. When our eyes met, I all but drowned in the emerald sea of hers, until a sharp pain at the base of my hump reminded me of the heavy strain I was putting it under, holding the beam up above my head. I let it drop in front of me. The loud thump startled Esmeralda, whose dreamy expression gave way to one of fear as she finally understood what I was.

It hurt more than I would ever admit. And it hurt even more when her eyes further widened at the sight of my hump. Now that my arms were down, this bane of my existence forced me into this hunched over, servile position. Anger and shame filled my heart.

"You shouldn't be here," I grumbled, when in truth, my fingers ached to reach out and touch her perfect, golden skin.

"Why?" Esmeralda asked in a soft voice, instead of the apology followed by a quick exit I had expected.

I looked at her in surprise, oddly moved by her clearly attempting to silence her fear. My imps flying to her, each settling on one of Esmeralda's shoulders before kissing her cheek, kept me from answering. Although taken aback, she seemed more amused than distraught by their excessive display of affection.

"Lazarus, Victus, leave her be," I said in a stern voice.

They gave me a sheepish look and reluctantly flew over to settle on my own shoulders.

"I didn't mind," Esmeralda said, clasping her delicate hands in front of her.

"You should mind," I said in a harsher tone than I'd intended. "You're an Anointed. Your purity shouldn't be tainted by exposure to a Fallen and his familiars."

She raised a surprised eyebrow at me, then tilting her head to the side, the Vestal studied my features as if they could reveal some hidden mystery.

"Are you all suffering from some kind of contagious disease that could 'taint' my purity?" she asked in teasing tone that made my desire go up another notch.

"No, but the Praetor would be livid to know you are here," I countered, confused by her apparent desire to stay and converse with me.

To my shock, Esmeralda's face closed off, taking on a stern edge. "The Praetor doesn't own me. He doesn't get to dictate where I go or who I speak to."

"He intends to make you his bride," I said, jealousy and possessive anger seeping into my voice.

"Whatever his intentions, any such plans would be premature. I've only been here a day," she replied with a dismissive shrug. "Anyway, whether I marry him or another, I will be no man's property. If I choose to speak to someone, including a Fallen," she added with a meaningful look towards me, "it will be my choice and no one else's… Well, assuming said Fallen is okay to speak with me."

*Do I ever want to!*

Until now, besides my vague memory of an older human female who had raised me in my early childhood, Frollo and my imps were the only ones I had ever spoken with.

*And Frollo will skin me alive if he catches me with her.*

"You are the Blessed Esmeralda," I said mockingly, trying to hide how hungry I was for her presence and companionship. "Who wouldn't want to speak with you?"

She waved a dismissive hand. "That title is as much a burden as it is an honor. But right now, I'm simply Mera, freshly landed on the First Circle, and curious about its citizens; *all* of them."

"Then the first thing you should know, *Mera,* is that the humans of the First Circle, and especially on the outskirts of Paris, hate the Fallen with a passion," I said with a stern voice, in a final attempt to drive her away. "Aiding one to enter any human city, harboring one within their walls, or merely fraternizing with one could be considered as treason, a crime punishable by death. So, once again, for your own sake, you shouldn't be here."

"Is that what you want then? For me to leave?" she asked after a beat.

I flinched, biting my tongue not to shout for her to stay and never leave. Averting my eyes, I bent down to pick up the load-bearing beam for the roof of the outdoor forge I was building.

The imps flew off my shoulders, and Esmeralda gasped when I lifted it above my head in one swift movement.

"Careful!" she exclaimed. "That's too heavy!"

My eyes snapped down to meet hers, a sliver of anger rising within me. "I am a hunchback, not an invalid," I snarled.

Extending my arms as far up as possible, I carefully settled the load-bearing beam on top of the two vertical support beams that I had previously erected. Once secured, my gaze reconnected with Mera's, challenging her to doubt my abilities again. Being seen as less—seeing *myself* as less—because of my hump had always been my greatest weakness. However, I didn't so much mind being half-Fallen; no one controlled their genetics. But being a hunchback, even though I had no control over that, irrationally felt like a personal failure.

Instead of the embarrassed look I'd expected from her, Esmeralda merely bowed her head in concession, a glimmer of admiration in her stunning green eyes.

"I never considered you an invalid," she said in a soft voice with a hint of friendly mockery. "But I most certainly stand corrected regarding my assumptions about your strength. It is quite phenomenal."

My face heated, and I once more averted my eyes, not knowing how to handle a compliment—especially one coming from her. The teasing smile stretching her lips did strange things to me, and another wave of desire washed over me.

"Thank you," I mumbled, feeling too self-conscious to continue working. Yet, I wanted to keep going to both hide how overwhelmed I felt in her presence, and to keep my hands occupied so that they wouldn't reach out and grab her as they ached to do.

"You're welcome," she said, taking a few steps closer to the house, an unreadable look in her eyes. "But you still haven't answered my question."

"Why would you even want to stay here to speak with me?" I asked with a frown, genuinely confused by her persistence.

Esmeralda didn't answer right away, pondering the response she would give. "Honestly," she said at last, "because you intrigue me. Because I'm feeling a strange connection with you that I do not understand. And because, somehow, you enhance my power."

I gaped at her, taken aback by such candor, but also by the fact that she, too, felt the connection. The possessiveness she stirred within me grew another notch. It had to be a sign. But a sign of what? I could never have her. Had Esmeralda been a commoner, I could have absconded with her into the woods, beyond human and Fallen territories. However, she wasn't just a Vestal, which already made her untouchable, she was also Anointed.

"Last night, it was you on the balcony, right?" the Vestal asked, advancing by another step.

Fearing my voice would betray my emotions, I simply nodded in response.

"I recognize your energy. It made my Chant more powerful than I would have ever believed possible," she said pensively. "I didn't think Fallen also possessed that ability. But then, we never mingle with them, so it's no wonder no one noticed. Or did you inherit it from your human parent?"

"Also?" I asked, confused, ignoring her question.

"We have inherited our energy manipulation powers from the Elohim," Esmeralda patiently explained while advancing a couple more steps towards me. "They invited humans here when less and less of the original inhabitants of the Nine Circles were born with an affinity with energy manipulation. My ancestors were among the Chosen because females in my family responded well to the Elohim's ergokinetic influence. I have not personally experienced it… yet. Well, until you that is. But that is why the Seraphs always attend the Festival of Light ceremony;

their power enhances the Vestal's and increases the chances of filling the Well."

"I see," I said, suddenly ashamed by my limited knowledge of the inner workings of the rituals of the city I had grown up in.

It stung a little that her interest in me only stemmed from my apparently innate ability to make her more powerful, and not out of some deeper attraction or care for me. Still, I welcomed her attention, whatever motivated it. There would be plenty of time later to pay the price when Frollo inevitably found out about this encounter.

"I am also glad to see you are well," Esmeralda added, as if she'd read the thoughts that had just crossed my mind. "You sounded… indisposed."

I squirmed under her inquisitive stare and ran a nervous hand through my midnight blue hair. "Thank you, I am fine now." Her intense gaze on me clearly indicated she expected more details. For some reason, I felt compelled to show her the same candor she had shown me. "I have a condition which builds up over a month and causes me great pain. The Praetor regularly helps me with it, as he did last night."

Her gaze lowered to my shoulder as if she could see my hump beyond it, a small frown marring her delicate forehead.

"It pleases me to hear Frollo assisted you. He seemed quite… upset."

"I shouldn't have been there," I replied, my voice hardening. "It was foolish of me to put him and myself in danger by risking discovery." My gaze bore into hers so there would be no misunderstanding this time about my meaning. "If my presence was exposed, my life would likely be forfeit, and the Praetor could face a world of trouble for having harbored a Fallen."

"You are only half-Fallen," she argued, studying my features. "Technically, that part of you should give you some rights. But I get your meaning well. Your secret is safe with me."

I nodded in gratitude, but my lack of a sense of relief made me realize I'd never doubted she wouldn't expose us.

Watching Esmeralda chew her bottom lip as she hesitated to ask me the next question burning her tongue reignited the flame of desire that had dimmed to slow-burning embers.

"You may ask your question. I have no secrets," I said.

She raised a dubious eyebrow, and my cheeks heated, realizing I still hadn't answered her initial question. Thankfully, Esmeralda let me off the hook on that one.

"Have you considered seeking medical attention? There are treatments for kyphosis—I mean, hunched backs—like special braces or even surgery."

The timid way she asked the question, clearly trying not to hurt my feelings, deeply touched me. I wasn't used to anyone worrying about my sensibilities. Frollo wasn't cruel per se, merely indifferent, which made it all the harder for me to understand why he'd put himself at such high risk for so many years to provide me with shelter and succor. The only other people in the temple aware of my nature were his two personal guards, Ulrich and Gareth. I'd never conversed with them, but they'd barked a couple of orders at me in the past. This made me all the hungrier for pleasant conversation with her.

"It is not possible," I said, shaking my head. "We had tried a brace when I was a child. It nearly killed me. Frollo… I mean Praetor Frollo had procured a handheld scanner to see what was wrong with my hump. The experts he brought the readings to all had the same verdict. The explanation he gave me had been too complex for my young mind at the time. But it came down to the need for surgery to fix it. A *major* surgery, which couldn't be performed by one or two highly trusted people in some backwoods shack. Since then, he has been alleviating my pains, and even built a laboratory on the third floor of the spire to further his medical knowledge and better assist me."

The stunned then impressed look on her face highly

displeased me. Although Frollo deserved my gratitude for the lengths he'd gone to for me, I didn't want to sing his praises to Esmeralda, and further push her into his arms.

"I had no idea Frollo was so devoted to your care," she said pensively. "It is an unexpected but very nice side of him I never would have foreseen." Her gaze roamed over the house before settling on me again. "Tell me about this place."

Too happy for the conversation to steer away from Frollo's virtues, I gladly gave her a tour of the house, bigger than my loft at the top of the spire. Even without the breathtaking view of Paris of my previous place, I still had large windows in every room, using reflective glass so that a passerby could not peek inside or catch a glimpse of me—not that anyone ever came to this area.

My greatest pride, however, was showing her my armory with a collection of lances, spears, staves, and bows. Although self-taught, I'd always had an innate talent for the craft. The look of wonder on her face touched me more than any word she could have said.

"This one is similar to the lightning staves the guards were holding upon my arrival," Esmeralda exclaimed.

I puffed out my chest further. "It is, because I made their staves based on that template. I make most of the ceremonial weapons for the Praetor."

"That's amazing!" she said with awe. "You are incredibly talented."

In my enthusiasm at her positive response, I launched into a detailed description of each weapon, their meaning, inspiration, material, and technique used. I'd never had anyone but my imps to speak with of my passion, and the flood gates were now wide open. I eventually realized I was babbling and abruptly shut up, feeling mortified.

Far from looking bored or annoyed, Esmeralda chuckled, her beautiful emerald eyes sparkling with mirth.

"It is wonderful to see someone feeling such passion about things they do," she said in a sympathetic voice. "Listening to you reminds me of how I feel when I dance or Chant. Don't you dare be embarrassed about loving what you do. Your enthusiasm is contagious. Thank you for giving me this window into your world."

More embarrassed than ever, I didn't quite know what to do with myself. "Thank you for being such a great listener," I replied, lamely.

She smiled and performed a little curtsey. "I should probably get going," Esmeralda said. "I wouldn't want to overstay my welcome considering you never officially gave me permission to stay," she added teasingly.

I mumbled something lame about it having been no bother, my chest tightening at the thought I might never see her again, or at least, not like this. For a little while, I'd almost forgotten about the hostile world outside that I'd never belong to. It had only been her and me, and the pesky imps.

Moving out of her way, I schooled my features not to show how crestfallen I felt at her imminent departure, and let her exit the armory—the only mostly furnished room in my cabin. The guards would bring the rest of my belongings either tomorrow or the day after.

Feeling like a lost puppy, I escorted her in silence to the hidden path through the hedges. She stopped, turned to look at me, and smiled at Victus who had just landed on my shoulder.

"It was lovely meeting you…?"

The look she gave me implied a question. I blinked, not knowing what she wanted.

"It was a pleasure meeting you, too," I said in a hesitant voice.

Esmeralda's smile broadened, and she looked at me as if I'd said something cute. "I was hoping you'd tell me your name, since you already know mine."

"Oh! Right. Kwazeem. My name is Kwazeem," I said, feeling more idiotic than ever—if not borderline rude. But then, no one had ever cared to know my name. This socializing thing was proving quite challenging. "Apologies."

"No need to apologize," she said in a gentle voice. "Kwazeem is a lovely name; unusual, but lovely," Mera added while giving me an assessing look. "Would it be okay for me to occasionally visit you again in the future?"

*YES!*

I barely managed not to shout out the word as my chest filled with so much joy I feared it would burst. Yet, the suddenly shy and uncertain look on her face, and the adorable pink creeping on her cheeks made me think it had been a bold request on her part, which only got me even more excited.

*But Frollo will banish you.*

I shouldn't. I knew better. But Esmeralda was mine. Every cell in my body screamed as much. Whatever the consequences, I couldn't—wouldn't—miss a chance. The connection between us was undeniable, and she felt it, too.

"My home is your home," I said, carefully. "But remember that the Praetor will be furious if he finds out that you do."

A strange expression crossed her features, before they took on an air of determination. "Leave the Praetor to me," Esmeralda said in a severe tone. "I am not his property, and you are not his slave. He cannot dictate who I can be friends with. So, I will see you soon, Kwazeem."

Holding back the stupid grin that wanted to plaster itself on my face, I nodded and replied, "See you soon, Mera."

She beamed at me hearing me say her nickname, then turned around and left. Long after Esmeralda had vanished from view, I stood at the edge of the hidden pathway with that stupid grin.

# CHAPTER 6
## ESMERALDA

Waking up this morning and finding out there would be no Chakra ceremonies this week was the best news Frollo could have given me. There was no way I could have focused on dozens of people more interested in gawking at the new Vestal in town than in aligning the energy of their Chakras. And I wouldn't even mention the most beautiful forbidden fruit I'd ever laid eyes on.

Kwazeem was pure perfection.

I didn't hate the Fallen. The Fifth Circle—the dark moon on which I grew up—had no quarrel with those that inhabited it. They kept to their lands and even traded with us. Truth be told, I'd always found them rather attractive the few times I'd managed to get a glimpse of them. Then again, considering the unappealing other choices in Obscura, anything else could only be better. But I genuinely loved Kwazeem's bluish-grey skin, shiny scales my fingers had itched to touch, and those lovely horns on his forehead. However, it was his gorgeous, silver eyes that had fascinated me the most... Well, okay, after his plump lips that I'd been dying to kiss.

But meeting him in the flesh had raised even more questions

than before. If he was to be believed—and I had no reason to doubt Kwazeem's words—Frollo was taking a huge risk granting him asylum on the temple's grounds and within the walls of Paris. I didn't know the Praetor well enough, yet my every instinct told me that he wasn't one to put himself in jeopardy out of altruism towards those in need. He was fiercely ambitious and had effectively reached the highest administrative rank possible in Eden before reaching the age of forty. Why put all of that on the line for a Fallen hybrid?

There had to be something in it for him. But what?

And then why did their energy feel so similar? The signature was almost identical, a phenomenon I'd only ever witnessed in twins.

*Could they be siblings?*

The thought gave me pause. They were both stunningly gorgeous. And although they didn't look alike, their faces both had angelic features, and their heights matched that of an Elohim offspring. Is that what it was? Had Frollo's mother committed an indiscretion with a Fallen and asked her firstborn to look after his youngest sibling? Vestals all had some degree of divine blood, and a recessive gene could have manifested in both her offspring.

My mind latched on to that theory, turning it in every angle to see if it held water.

But why had I felt such an unbridled, animal desire for Frollo yesterday morning, but only a fiercely possessive attraction towards Kwazeem? My body's reaction to the Praetor had felt like a betrayal. With his 'gardener,' it had felt just right, although underwhelming in its intensity.

That, too, confused me.

It was like between the day of my arrival in Paris and the following morning, they had swapped their powers. Because there was no question Frollo's power hadn't been particularly remarkable that first day, whereas Kwazeem had elevated mine like never before. And now this?

There was something strange going on, and I would get to the bottom of it.

For now, having been spared breakfast with Frollo—who had Praetor duties to attend—I wandered the streets of Paris, bustling with activity as the citizens frantically prepared for the Festival. A construction crew had begun building a massive dais near the landing pad where guests of honor—including High Seraph Phoebus—would sit during my performance. All around the plaza, surrounding the Well of Power, tall poles with a cushion at the top had been erected. It took me a second to realize they were extra seats for the additional Elohim who might attend and not have a seat at the main table.

The Elohim didn't mingle with common mortals. After a few minutes of sustained exposure, the constant aura of energy emanating from them would indispose anyone with no affinity with ergokinesis, which meant the majority of the population.

More workers toiled assembling multiple long tables along the edges of the plaza, where a giant buffet would be laid out for the citizens to partake in the free feast of the Festival of Light. Over the centuries, the Festival had become a mish-mash of pagan rituals. While its true purpose was merely to refill the Well of Power so that the city and its dependencies would have electrical power for the next three to six months, other more exciting celebrations had been tacked on to it.

In its symbolism, the Festival would bring light to chase away darkness, and with it, the demons that lurked within. The population would therefore don disguises of monsters, fearsome creatures, or loose representations of things that terrify people such as death, diseases, poverty, etc. Even now, many of the stands in the open market had a plethora of costume offerings. I slowed down to examine them, in particular the masks, each more creative than the other. Knowing I had no personal use for a costume, the merchants thankfully let me be, content to give me a polite smile while ogling me with curiosity. Constantly being observed by multiple pairs of eyes could get a little irritating, but at least they didn't bother me with unnecessary inane conversations.

The almost recluse-like life of endless training on Obscura had made me a bit of an introvert.

I stopped dead in my tracks upon reaching the fourth stall, coming face to face with the most stunningly realistic Fallen mask. It came with two options for the outfit; either a long, hooded robe, or a holographic suit that created an illusion of their greyish-blue skin and scales. Fascinated, I walked up to it and ran my fingertips over the beautiful dark-grey horns on the mask.

"Beautiful, isn't it?" asked a woman's voice behind me.

Startled, my head jerked to the left, looking at her over my shoulder. In her mid-fifties, black hair streaked with a few strands of silver held in a bun, the woman's hazel eyes stared at me with an unreadable expression.

"Yes," I said. "It's quite stunning and incredibly realistic."

The woman, who visibly ran the stall, came to stand next to me and touched the silvery scales alongside the jaw of the Fallen. Kwazeem didn't have scales there but some kind of bony spikes with rounded tips that I'd been dying to touch as well.

"Althea—commonly referred to as Old Nan or 'the Hag' by the less respectful youth—made it, along with the seven other masks you see here," the merchant said, waving at them.

They were all just as flawlessly made, all of them representing real life entities deemed dangerous and fearsome by the locals. But unlike the other masks I had seen in previous stalls, hers didn't depict them as grotesque. Her work struck me as respectful towards them.

"Her work is phenomenal. But this one remains my favorite," I said with sincerity, my gaze returning to the Fallen.

"A Vestal drawn to a Fallen. Beware, child," the merchant said with a knowing smile. "For some reason, their kind holds a strong appeal for yours when you are in fact meant for the Elohim. Be careful that you do not fall alongside them."

"Fall?" I asked, taken aback by that comment.

"The few Vestals who have allowed themselves to be seduced by those creatures have lost their powers, their affinity with ergokinesis permanently severed," the woman said in a slightly dramatic way. "They were driven out of town in shame and cast out as pariahs. The only reason they weren't executed was because the law forbids raising a hand against an ordained Vestal, even one on whom Vesta herself has turned her back."

That winded me. I had never heard of Vestals losing their powers, and we'd never been warned against fraternizing with the Fallen. It had been a given that any of us who became ordained would be paired with an Elohim, a Praetor, or one of the high magistrates of the Circle we would be assigned to.

"Are you sure they are draining the powers of the Vestal?" I asked, dubiously. "Before the divine wars, before they became the Fallen, the Light Bearers used to enhance the powers of the Elohim."

"They did," the woman conceded. "But they also fed from their energy. Why do you think that, aside from Vestals, common humans can no longer live on Elysium? Without the Light Bearers to absorb the excess energy swirling around them, the Elohim—especially the Seraphs—might as well be nuclear power cores with wings. In fact, before the Fall, the Fallen were equally called Light Bearers and Light Eaters."

Obviously, I was aware of that part. With female births among Elohim being extremely low, it explained why many of their males attended a new Vestal's first Festival of Light to find out if she could be their soulmate. But only a few of us received that honor. As an Anointed, the Matriarchs at the temple on Obscura where I'd been raised were holding high hopes that I would not only be one of the chosen, but that my mate would be one of the most powerful Elohim of Elysium. Some going so far as betting I would be High Seraph Phoebus's mate.

I had hoped so as well. But now that I'd met a certain hybrid, my whole world had been turned upside down. I barely knew him, and yet…

"Since the Fall, the light of the Elohim has died within the Fallen," the merchant continued. "Now, they hunger for it. And this is why they are banned from our cities. They suck the light out of any offspring that could become a Vestal, and turn your Vestal sisters into commoners. Involuntarily though it may be, they would cast us into darkness if allowed near us. And yet, how beautiful is the beast?"

She added that last sentence in an almost wistful way. I suddenly wondered if she had personally known or been attracted to a Fallen. Could her stern warning be fueled by bitterness? As much as her arguments couldn't be dismissed, my experience with Kwazeem had been the direct opposite. He'd enhanced my power like never before, and part of that still lingered.

"Very," I whispered in a non-committal way. "I would like to buy this, with both the cloak and the holographic suit," I said, taken by a sudden whim. Having always been a by-the-book kind of woman, this new impulsive, almost impetuous side of me was disconcerting.

The female merchant recoiled, her eyes widening in shock. "*You* want to buy a costume?"

"It's not for me," I explained quickly. "But I have a friend whom I think might enjoy it."

She narrowed her eyes suspiciously at me but didn't pry further. Good for her, too, because I wouldn't have welcomed further intrusion into my personal business. While I considered myself a generally nice person, my claws swiftly came out when anyone thought to bully or control me.

"What else does Old Nan make?" I asked casually after paying her.

"Wild fruit preserves, scented candles, and natural body wash," the woman responded while wrapping my purchase.

I gaped at her, and she burst out laughing before extending me the bag containing the items I'd bought.

"She lives alone, deep in the Godswood," the merchant explained. "Despite her age, that stubborn old woman is self-sufficient, and makes most of the things she needs on the day to day. She rarely sells for currency, preferring to trade for the things she cannot make. For this, however," she said pointing at my bag with her chin, "Old Nan will take her share in credits."

"Thank you, Madam," I said politely. "This was most informative."

"Please, call me Ellen," the merchant said. "You will soon find out that, despite all appearances, Paris is quite informal."

"Well then, thank you, Ellen," I said with a smile.

"My pleasure, Vestal Esmeralda."

I left her stall having lost any further desire to shop or wander around. Too many new questions swirled in my head. How in the world had Kwazeem come to be in Frollo's care? Who was his mother? Why did he enhance me rather than drain me?

More than ever, the theory of them being siblings seemed credible. I needed to dig into Frollo's past and that of the previous Vestals who had come to Paris. It was common practice for a Vestal who didn't marry her current Praetor to rotate between cities and moons in the hopes of finding her match. Therefore, keeping track of a Vestal's whereabouts would be no small task, especially considering the swaps were often agreed upon merely between the Praetors and Vestals involved. It was an informal practice not strictly controlled.

Back on Obscura, once I'd been ordained, my profile had gone up on the registry and every interested Praetor sent me an invitation. I merely picked the most appealing one. Should the day come when I decided to leave Paris, I could simply either put my name back up in the registry or directly contact the Praetor whose temple I wanted to serve and hope he would accept. Naturally, a Vestal couldn't leave her temple until a replacement for her had been found.

I didn't quite know where to start. Interrogating Kwazeem on the previous Vestals might tip him off. And asking Frollo might give him the wrong impression I felt jealous of them. My complete absence of possessiveness towards him spoke volumes as to the fact we would never be a match. Sure, I found him physically attractive, and my body had reacted strangely to his energy, but I believed it was merely because it felt so strongly like Kwazeem's. Furthermore, knowing he'd been taking turns with the Maidens did nothing to endear him to me. My lack of jealousy there as well confirmed there was no future for us. The mere thought of one of the Maidens drooling over my Kwazeem made me want to commit murder.

*My Kwazeem...*

Despite his efforts to hide his attraction, it had been plain to see on his face, reflecting my own. So many times, his fingers had twitched as he clearly fought the urge to reach out and touch me. I wished he would have given in. Then again, how would I have reacted if he had?

*You know very well how you would have reacted.*

My cheeks heated at the thought. A few passersby gave me a knowing smile, which only embarrassed me further, but this time with a tinge of humiliation. It didn't take a genius to know they were assuming naughty thoughts involving the Praetor had crossed my mind. All of them likely believed he and I had been doing the deed since my arrival, two days ago.

How wrong they were.

But that did give me an idea. The Maidens and I would be practicing the Chant again in a couple of hours from now. Most of them were gossips from whom I could gather some intel, and all of them still foolishly hoped to shackle the Praetor. It had taken me a minute to realize a man of his ambition would never settle for a female that couldn't further his status. These Maidens were too weak, having been flunked out of Obscura's temple in their early teens for failing to achieve high enough power. As cruel as that sounded, they would always play second violin to a Vestal.

Relieved to leave the prying eyes of the crowd behind, I entered the shelter of the temple only to find Frollo getting off the lift and marching towards me. I groaned inwardly but plastered a friendly smile on my face as I met him halfway. The same magnetic aura emanated from him. However, while my body responded with lust again, this time, I realized it wasn't lust *for him*. Frollo's aura awakened my senses and made me itch for release, but my mind was dampening the mindless frenzy I'd felt yesterday morning. Even though my nipples hardened and racy images popped into my head, they featured a male with a much different face than the Praetor's.

"Hello, Mera. Sorry for missing you this morning," Frollo said, with his signature suave expression.

Refraining from rolling my eyes, I couldn't comprehend how the Maidens could fall for it. Worse still, I regretted my eagerness in letting him call me Mera. On his lips, it almost felt dirty.

"No need to apologize. You're a busy man with far too many responsibilities to also burden yourself with looking after me," I said sympathetically. "And it's not like your beautiful city doesn't have plenty to keep oneself occupied."

"So I see. You've been shopping?" he asked, although his question was more of a statement as he eyed my bag meaningfully.

My stomach dropped. Although I owed him no explanation about my comings and goings, I didn't want Kwazeem to get in trouble over me visiting him.

"I have," I said evasively.

The silence stretched, becoming slightly uncomfortable as he waited in vain for me to go into further details.

"I hope you found all that you were looking for," he finally said, his tone slightly clipped.

"I have. That open market is wonderful," I said, relieved to move the topic in a different direction. "If the temple's chef wasn't so amazing, I would have bought a little of everything out there. The cakes and pastries on offering in Paris are out of this world!"

Praise for his city appeared to mollify him slightly. "They most certainly are. Wait until you see the decadent buffet that will be served at the Festival of Light," he boasted.

I smiled, genuinely excited. "The construction work is advancing well. I can't wait to see the final version."

"Friday, in the wee hours of the morning, well before sunrise, bioluminescent plants will ornate the plaza," Frollo said, with an excitement similar to mine. "Once they begin to glow in the day's fading light, it will be your turn to light up the city."

My heart skipped a beat, torn between anxiety and anticipation. But a different thought dominated my mind.

"Is your gardener going to take care of that?" I asked innocently, jumping on the opening he had unwittingly provided me.

Frollo stiffened, his gaze narrowing, looking for a deceit I worked hard to dissimulate. "Yes," he replied with a curt tone, his face losing all warmth and enthusiasm.

"That's amazing. It sounds like a lot of work for a single person. Then again, I visited the temple's garden yesterday, and it's quite stunning. I'm assuming he recovered well from whatever ailed him two nights ago?"

"My gardener is fine. You do not need to concern yourself with him," he bit out, his voice becoming icy enough to freeze the sun.

"Why are you so angry?" I challenged in a soft voice. "I do

not mind if he or any of the staff wishes to listen in when we rehearse the Chant. It is only when I practice the dance to Vesta that I require privacy. Please, do not be mad at him over a little curiosity."

"My gardener is here under specific terms, and he violated them yesterday," Frollo snapped. "He suffers a particular condition which makes him dangerous to himself and potentially to others. There's a reason he remains out of sight and works at hours that reduce the possibility of him running into anyone. Your compassion and empathy honor you, but for his sake—and all of ours—do not seek him out. Should you cross paths with him, turn around and go the other way. Do not encourage him to further put himself at risk."

"I understand," I said with pretend submission. "I am relieved he has you to look after him. No one should be alone."

Frollo harrumphed, looking mightily uncomfortable. "Well, I must be on my way. I'm afraid I won't be able to enjoy your delectable company until late tomorrow evening. Hopefully, you can join me for dinner."

"Until tomorrow then," I said with a smile.

Frollo bowed his head then walked out of the temple. His two personal guards that I hadn't noticed until now standing by the door, quietly shadowed him. Heaving a sigh, both in relief and confusion, I headed to my room to prepare for the Chant.

# CHAPTER 7
## KWAZEEM

Thrusting, spinning, and swiping, I repeated the combat moves the city guards regularly performed on their training ground. It saddened me that I would no longer be able to look upon them from my former loft at the top of the spire. I loved combat. Despite my misshapen form, my body felt like it had been made specifically for that. My movements flowed effortlessly as if no hump sought to restrain them.

But today, I fought with an energy fueled by an underlying anger. Two days had gone by since Esmeralda's first visit. Two long days since she'd asked if she could visit me again. Granted, the Vestal had not specified when or how frequently she would, but my heart ached and longed for her presence. A million horrible images of her succumbing to Frollo's charms constantly flashed through my mind, further fueling my rage.

I was more isolated than ever; far worse than I had anticipated.

Even my imps felt it. They'd become my only eyes on what was happening in the rest of the world. But they needed to be extra careful during the day, not to be spotted. This was all my stupid fault, too. If only I had resisted the urge to go listen to her Chant.

*Then, she would never have visited you here.*

However, what was the point of that first visit if it were to be the last?

In an access of rage, I swiped my staff with all my strength in three quick successions at a large tree in the clearing next to my house. Then, with a war cry, I spun on myself, to strike it again using my momentum.

"Whatever that tree did to you, I apologize on its behalf."

Startled, my head jerked left to look over my shoulder at the distant voice I'd been dreaming about. My heart, already pounding from the effort, picked up another notch. Breathing heavily, I gaped at the vision of perfection that gracefully approached me with feline steps. Dressed all in white with a simple bandeau top and a flowy skirt with a thigh-high slit on the side, Esmeralda looked good enough to eat. Her cute belly button exposed above the low line of her skirt begged to be nibbled and sucked on. And that golden-brown skin made my mouth water.

I'd been so lost in my jealous and hurt rage that I'd not felt her energy slowly seeping into me as she made her approach.

"It did nothing," I mumbled, feeling suddenly self-conscious to be naked but for the tight shorts I'd been wearing. "It's just my regular training routine."

"You're impressive," Esmeralda said.

The way her gaze briefly roamed over me hinted at more than just my combat skills. My face heated, and I glanced down at my body slick with sweat.

"Thank you," I said, running nervous fingers through my damp hair. "This is an unexpected surprise. Had I known such pleasant company was coming, I would have been in a less offensive accoutrement."

This time, Esmeralda gave me a slow, deliberate once over that had my blood boiling with need and my throat going dry.

"Do I look offended to you?" she asked in a sultry voice, her green eyes darkening.

I opened and closed my mouth a few times, words failing me. My imps rushing towards Esmeralda to peck her cheeks, then immediately flying off before I could chastise them, spared me from answering. She laughed as they settled on one of the lowest branches of the tree I'd been brutally venting my frustration on.

Still smiling, Esmeralda closed the distance between us. "I hope you haven't eaten yet," she said, showing me a basket I hadn't even noticed her holding. I'd been so enthralled by her beauty and at having her here with me again that nothing else had mattered. "I brought breakfast for us and a present for you."

My brain froze, struggling to process all she had just said. As far as I could recall, I'd never received a present. But, more importantly, we would share a meal together. This meant she would stay with me for at least thirty minutes. Could I dare hope longer even? Esmeralda raising a perfect eyebrow questioningly snapped me out of my dazed trance.

"No, I have not," I said, relieved that my voice came out firmer than I'd expected. "I would love to share a meal with you. But first, I should clean up."

"Wonderful!" Esmeralda exclaimed, her stunning eyes sparkling with joy. That did something to me that I couldn't explain, but that I wanted more of. "Where would you like to eat? Inside your house, or a picnic on the grass?"

I'd never had a picnic before, not in the traditional sense and in good company. I opened my mouth to choose that option, but the sight of her pristine white skirt made me hesitate.

Catching me frowning at her skirt, Esmeralda immediately understood my dilemma. "Do not worry about my skirt. I brought a picnic blanket, just in case," she said, puffing out her chest proudly.

I beamed at her, feeling like a child having been handed a bag full of sweets. "Then a picnic would be great," I said. "I know just the place, too. I often eat there, by the river. After training, I normally bathe there then eat something sitting under a pear tree near the water."

"Sounds perfect!" Esmeralda said with enthusiasm. "Lead the way!"

I suddenly felt intimidated at the thought of turning my back on her, which would put my bare hump in plain sight. Sure, she'd already kind of seen it, but it was with me in a flurry of movements. Now, she'd get an up-close view of my deformity.

"You can go on ahead," I said with false enthusiasm. "It's straight ahead, down that trail. I'll go grab a change of clothes and catch up with you."

Heat crept up my cheeks knowing I hadn't fooled her in the least. But instead of calling me out on my cowardice, Esmeralda smiled gently, and nodded, playing along.

"See you soon then," she said, before turning around and walking down the path.

I ran into the house and picked up a flowy black shirt and a pair of loose black pants. A part of me wished I could don one of the tight shirts I usually wore when blacksmithing as they nicely hugged the muscles of my abs and chest—which I was quite proud of. But they also outlined my hump too much. What I wouldn't give to simply be able to slice it off. After grabbing a smart washcloth, I rushed back out of the house in a jog to catch up with my woman.

"All set?" she asked as I adjusted my step to hers.

"Yes," I replied with a smile, freeing her of the picnic basket. It proved surprisingly heavy, which made me all the more curious as to its contents.

Guessing where we were headed, my imps flew past us in a cacophony of happy chirps, doing aerial acrobatics in front of us.

Esmeralda burst out laughing at their antics, making me grin in turn. In that instant, I felt happy and carefree; emotions I couldn't recall ever experiencing before filling me.

On instinct, my free hand reached out for hers. Panic set in when I realized, too late, what I'd done. Electric coils swirled around our joined hands for a second before fading. Esmeralda's lips parted with a discreet gasp. Her steps faltered so briefly I wondered if I'd imagined it. Bracing for her to recoil in disgust or scold me harshly for daring to touch a Vestal without her express consent, I cast a wary look towards her. Esmeralda looked up at me, a sweet, almost shy smile blossoming on her lips. Rather than pulling out of my grasp, her hand tightened around mine.

Despite the energy coursing between us through our connected hands, and the fierce attraction I felt for her, it wasn't lust that dominated my current emotions; just joy in its purest form. And gratitude...

For the first time, the trickling sound of the running river getting stronger saddened me. I didn't want to let go of Esmeralda's hand any time soon, if ever. With much reluctance, I released her after indicating an ideal little plateau created by a large, flat rock by the river. A tall tree with a thick trunk next to it would partially hide me from view while I bathed.

"I'll be swift," I said, feeling more self-conscious than ever.

"Take your time. I have no plans for the rest of the day," Esmeralda said.

My heart leaped in my chest at the underlying meaning of her words. With Frollo out of town, I effectively could keep her all to myself for an entire day. Wanting to make the most of that precious gift, I nodded and hurried to the other side of the tree, walking as straight as my hump allowed without making it too obvious.

The weight of her stare burned holes in my back until I broke her line of sight by moving around the tree. I put down my bundle of fresh clothes, quickly discarded the ones on me, and then ran into the river. The cold water bit into my flesh and made my half-erect shaft want to curl in on itself. And yet, it failed to cool the fire in my veins. What I wouldn't have given for Esmeralda to be right here in the water with me, her golden body pressed against mine.

I had touched Mera, and she had welcomed it.

That thought boggled my mind. I frantically rubbed myself with the smart washcloth, eager to get back to my woman. Even as I washed myself, the memory of her soft hand in mine was messing with my head. She'd looked happy about the bold way in which I'd just claimed it and had allowed such brazen behavior. Esmeralda genuinely seemed to enjoy my company… to like me.

*And I want her to like me even more.*

A million thoughts crossed my mind as I mentally inventoried all the things we could do, the topics we could discuss, the places around Paris that I could safely show her. But one thought kept interfering with my more rational meanderings: how could I get to touch her again?

Making quick work of my ablutions, I hurried out of the water to the 'safe' side of the large tree. While in the water, the nanites of the smart washcloth had worked on removing dirt and dead skin from my body, wherever I rubbed it. Now, out of water, it absorbed all the surface moisture on me to help dry me faster. A part of me, turned on at finding myself entirely naked with only a large tree between us, wanted to prolong the exquisite torture of having her so close and so vulnerable. The other part was utterly terrified she would somehow get a glimpse and be repulsed.

*Are similar thoughts of my nakedness crossing her mind?*

That she could potentially be fantasizing about me in this compromising position had my shaft instantly reawakened. My physical response to Esmeralda shamed me. She was stunningly beautiful, and the mere sight of her made my blood turn to liquid fire. But I wanted to believe that I wasn't so shallow. The powerful emotions that seized me in her presence couldn't be purely driven by lust. Every other Vestal who had stayed in Our Lady of Paris, each more attractive than the other, had left me indifferent. No, some deeper feelings and a far more meaningful connection existed between us, despite the primal urges Esmeralda awakened in me.

I swiftly donned my loose garments before stepping around the tree to join Esmeralda. The beaming smile she greeted me with had the most exquisite heat blossoming in the pit of my stomach and spreading throughout my body, but especially in my chest. Sitting on the blue picnic mat, her legs folded on the side, with her reddish-brown hair draped around her, she looked like a wood nymph waiting for her lover.

*How I wish...*

The most delectable-looking spread had been laid out on the mat in front of her, but in a way that only left room for me to sit right next to her. As if to confirm it had been intentional, she patted the mat next to her.

"I don't know what you like eating, so I brought a mix of everything," Esmeralda said.

"I am not picky," I said truthfully, "and this is quite a feast."

My mouth watered at the sight of fancy cold cuts, cheeses, breads, jams, sautéed potatoes, and sliced hot meats. I didn't know the name of half of the food in front of me, but it all looked divine. Frollo had not starved me in any way, but he'd never provided me with particularly fancy meals. I usually had a portion of the staff meals set aside for me—although I suspected the cook gave me the leftovers. You didn't save the finest pieces for a faceless employee no one had ever seen. As I grew older, I'd begun fishing and hunting and now have my pick of the prime pieces instead.

"Good! Dig in," Esmeralda said.

Picking up a warm loaf of multigrain bread, she broke it in half and extended one of them to me. I gratefully took it and imitated her as she slathered some dark blue jam on a piece before eating it. My taste buds nearly had an orgasm when the sweet flavors of blackberries, slightly spiced, invaded my mouth. I realized I'd probably moaned when Esmeralda giggled while staring at me, before tossing a piece of cheese in her mouth.

Naturally, my two imps parked themselves at the edge of the mat, looking at us with their irresistible big, black, needy eyes. Between two bites, Esmeralda fed them each a little bit of food, further increasing the tender emotions I felt for her.

"So, tell me about yourself," I asked. "How did you end up a Vestal?"

"The same boring way as everyone else, I'm afraid," she said modestly. "I was born on the Fourth Circle, the only girl and youngest of four siblings. My parents were fairly poor farmers and had hoped for a daughter that would qualify as a Vestal. Did they *ever* get their wish."

I raised a questioning eyebrow, nonetheless relieved at the absence of bitterness or anger in her voice.

"Every child is tested for ergokinesis at the age of five, both males and females, but we are the ones that really matter," Esmeralda explained. "If a male shows great potential for power, he would be trained in administration and law to possibly become a Praetor—although energy manipulation isn't a requirement for that role. But if a girl shows potential, her family receives a first dowry when she is taken to Obscura to begin her Vestal training. We have ten stages to complete in the twenty years of our training, the last one consisting of us being ordained. For each stage, another dowry is paid to our parents, the amount scaled according to our power level."

"So the more powerful you are, the more credits your parents receive?" I asked before taking a bite out of a juicy cube of some kind of red meat.

"Correct," Esmeralda said with a proud nod. "My dowries have taken my family out of poverty and into a comfortable life. With me being Anointed, my parents received a major bonus which has allowed them to buy additional lands and chattel. And that also enabled them to give each of my brothers a large enough plot of land to raise their own families."

"That's great," I said, although not quite comfortable with that system.

"You seem troubled," she said.

I hesitated, not wanting to appear judgmental or to make her feel as if I was devaluing her accomplishments.

"It's just… Hmmm, how do you feel about that?"

"I do not feel exploited, if that's what you're wondering," she said in a gentle voice. "And do not feel embarrassed for the thought crossing your mind. It is in fact a topic that surfaced often at the temple on Obscura among us the trainees. Some of my 'sisters' felt the dowry should have been set aside for us to enjoy once we'd been ordained. After all, *our* work was being rewarded."

"That is indeed what I was thinking," I admitted sheepishly.

"Which is fair. However, we have no use for those credits. Growing up on Obscura, our food and board was provided for," Esmeralda said, flicking her long hair over her bare shoulder. "And we only wore the uniforms given to us by the Matriarchs. Once we are ordained, the Circle whose invitation we accept pays us a large sign-on sum to spend on whatever we might see fit. But even then, as you can see here, food and lodging is free for us, so we have no real use for credits."

"I see what you mean," I replied pensively.

And I also could relate. Frollo didn't pay me wages for my gardening or blacksmithing work. It didn't bother me since he always provided me with any material things I might need upon request.

A wistful smile stretched her lips, and her eyes temporarily lost focus as she reminisced about something.

"It makes me happy knowing that doing what I love also gave my family a chance at the good life we otherwise never would have had," Esmeralda continued, refocusing on me. "I love my family. We don't see each other often, but those dowries allowed them to come visit me from time to time, which they couldn't have afforded otherwise. However, I understand the frustration of some of my Vestal sisters whose parents wasted their dowries on an extravagant lifestyle, well beyond their means, and who today have nothing to show for it. Before we were even ordained, some such parents were hinting that their daughters should continue to support them once they would start receiving their Vestal wages."

"I certainly hope your sisters will not," I said in a harsher tone than I'd intended.

Esmeralda chuckled, amused to see me so outraged on behalf of women I didn't know. "I hope not either," she replied after taking a sip of mulled wine. "I'm just grateful my parents' wise investment of my dowry has spared me having to face such unpleasantness. But enough about me, I'd love to hear about you."

My heart skipped a beat, suddenly feeling self-conscious all over again. Frollo wouldn't want me to speak to anyone about my past. Then again, he didn't want me to speak to anyone, which would include everyone but him.

"There isn't much to say about me," I said, squirming slightly under her intense gaze. "I was born in the Godswood. My mother passed away shortly thereafter due to complications with my birth. Had I been a 'normal' child, modern medicine would have saved her life, but…" I shrugged, trying to make light of the situation to hide the extent of the guilt I always felt at having 'killed' my mother. "I don't recall much of my youth, except for a cabin in the woods, near a river, and the constant smell of fresh breads and wild berries jam." I looked down at the almost empty jar of blackberry jam Esmeralda had brought, feeling somewhat embarrassed to have devoured most of it. I pointed at the jar with my index finger. "This reminds me of home. Or at least, of what had felt like home, even though the woman who had raised me there hadn't been my mother. But she had been kind."

"What was her name? And do you think you were related?" Esmeralda asked, her eyes sparkling with curiosity.

I shook my head. "I didn't know her name. Not her real name, at least. I called her Nan, as per her request. People would come to her shop, and I would hide in my room in the house while she traded with them. They called her Old Nan. I didn't think she was old but... What's wrong?" I asked, suddenly noticing the troubled expression on her face.

"It's just... Such an incredible coincidence," Esmeralda said hesitantly. "A few days ago, I met a merchant in town who told me about a woman named Althea—but commonly referred to as Old Nan—who lived in the woods and made beautiful costumes for the Festival, but mostly traded for jams and preserves. I had no idea it was the woman who had raised you! What happened? How did you end up here?"

"I became sick," I said glumly. "My condition started manifesting itself when I turned five; or rather, my hump did. Until then, I was a normal boy, running all over the place and being hyperactive. And then, the pain in my back grew more and more with the size of my hump. There were times I couldn't walk or get up."

"How terrible! I'm so sorry," Esmeralda said with a commiserating look on her beautiful face.

"It got better with time, in a way," I said with an 'it's okay' smile. The ease with which I was sharing this with her stunned me. I'd expected to be more self-conscious and embarrassed. "Nan would force me to get up, stretch, and exercise. Although my hump grew bigger, I adapted to its burden and to the way it restricted my movements.”

“I can only imagine how you might have been permanently crippled without her foresight,” Esmeralda said, a slight frown marring her forehead. “And I’m guessing she couldn’t call a doctor for you?”

I shook my head. “It would have put both of our lives in jeopardy. For the next couple of years, things were somewhat manageable. However, a month before my eighth birthday, things worsened. I started…”

The words died in my throat, and I cast a wary look in her direction. I was still ‘pretty’ for now, and would remain so for the next four to ten days to come. This was how I wanted her to see me, always. Should I tell her how ugly I became so early in whatever bond this was forming between us?

“It’s okay, Kwazeem. You can tell me anything,” she said gently, as if reading my thoughts.

I swallowed hard and nodded sharply. Delaying the inevitable would only make matters worse. If Esmeralda was going to turn her back on me because of my illness, as much as it would break me, I preferred she did it now than after a week of me misleading her.

“When my condition acts up,” I said in a slightly shaky voice, “my face and my hands swell disproportionately, and purplish blotches appear on my skin, as if I’d been in a bad fight. The pain in my back becomes pure agony.”

“Oh, Kwazeem,” Esmeralda said, her delicate palm settling on the back of my hand and giving it a gentle squeeze.

The same electric coils wrapped over our hands, swirling around our wrists before fading away. Still, Esmeralda’s energy seeped into me, stirring that odd power deep within me. It felt like the Light of the gods themselves had been lit inside my chest. Glorious and mighty, I wanted more of it. And yet, the moment it appeared, a familiar dull throbbing at the base of my hump manifested itself.

"It's okay," I repeated, covering her hand with my other one, both to increase the feel of her and to make sure she wouldn't pull away just yet. "It's in the past now. But back then, Nan and I both thought my days were numbered. She didn't say it, but I knew. For the next few weeks, she kept dosing me with poppy juice to keep me sedated so that I wouldn't spend my days screaming in pain. And then Frollo came to the cabin."

Esmeralda perked up, her stunning green eyes staring intently at me with burning curiosity. I hated that Frollo should have been the cause, but swallowed my jealousy.

"Most of that time is a blur to me. I was in too much pain and under too much sedation to truly understand what was going on," I said, gently caressing the back of her hand with my thumb, more to soothe myself than her. "Nan told me a man was working on a solution to help me, but I was too ill to make sense of anything. And then, one day, the pain was gone. My hump was bigger than ever, but the pain was gone. When it started to come back a couple of weeks later, Frollo came back, and continued to do so for the next three months until it was clear my condition would forever be recurring. That's when Nan said that I would be moving to the capital city to live with Frollo. I've been here ever since."

I said the last sentence with a shrug to hide the sadness constricting my throat. But that didn't fool my Esmeralda, who tightened her grip on my hand.

"Did you ever see Old Nan again?" she asked in a soft voice.

Not trusting my voice just yet, I shook my head and took in a couple of deep breaths. "The Godswood is too far if you aren't flying by shuttle. Going there would require me to cross Fallen territory on foot, and busy hunting grounds that would make it impossible for me not to be noticed, even if I traveled at night." I gazed upon Esmeralda's beautiful face, her coppery skin glowing under the soft rays of the sun piercing through the leaves of the tree. "Thank you for letting me know she's still well."

"Of course, Kwazeem. I wish I could tell you more. I…" Esmeralda's eyes suddenly widened as if she'd just remembered something. "Actually…"

To my chagrin, she pulled her hand from my grasp and reached for the bag which contained the gift she'd brought me. The loveliest pink crept up on Esmeralda's cheeks as she held the bag timidly in front of her almost like a shield.

"I saw this in one of the stalls in the marketplace, and it made me think of you. The craftsmanship is so exquisite, I couldn't help but buy it. Ellen—the merchant—told me Old Nan had made it. So, now it seems all the more predestined that I should have gotten it for you."

With a nervous laugh, Esmeralda extended the bag to me. Excitement and worry warred within me. I couldn't wait to see the gift, but her nervousness made me wonder at its nature. My blood froze at the sight of the life-like face of a Fallen staring back at me. A million thoughts pushed and shoved each other in my mind as I tried to make sense of that present.

"Is this how you see me?" I asked with tension in my voice. "As a Fallen?"

*As a monster?*

Esmeralda's gaze lost all nervousness, and she held mine with conviction. "I see you as a stunningly handsome man who happens to be half-human and half-Fallen. I am incredibly drawn to you, and I would love for you to come see me dance and Chant at the Festival in two days. So, I thought this costume fitting because I like you just the way you are, which includes your Fallen genetics. I also happen to think that costume is beautiful. That's all."

Each of her words felt like a balm on a wound I hadn't known plagued me. And yet, they caused something to snap deep within me; something wild, primal, and famished. Esmeralda's eyes widening with both shock and a sliver of fear made me realize I'd moved. With a speed that left me dizzy, I grabbed her by the shoulders and yanked her off the ground. Next thing I knew, she was standing, her back pressed against the tree, and my lips were claiming hers with brutal possessiveness.

Esmeralda stiffened, her hands fisting my shirt on my chest with a slight initial pushback. It quickly faded, and she relaxed against me, her arms wrapping around my neck. Too many sensations were crashing upon me to be able to compartmentalize them; the plush warmth of her lips against mine, her sweet and spicy taste laced with the mulled wine she'd drunk, the silkiness of her hair falling over my arms pinning her to the tree, the firm yet soft feel of her body and her full breasts pressing against my chest, and her hands... her divine hands touching me like no one ever has before.

A deep moan rose from my throat as the searing heat of Esmeralda's palms slipped under my flowy shirt to touch my skin directly. My abdominal muscles contracted almost painfully as her thumbs gently caressed the sides of my abs. But the exquisite torture didn't end as her hands roamed up to my chest, until the pads of her thumbs made their way to my nipples. My cock jerked in reaction at the unexpected sensual feel of her fingers circling them.

Esmeralda's lips parted, and my tongue invaded her mouth, hungry and demanding despite its clumsiness. My woman's own lack of experience only fueled my possessiveness and the need to brand her as mine. When my hands slipped under her chest bandeau, reciprocating her touch, Esmeralda moaned against my lips, reawakening that strange power within me.

Lowering her bandeau, I broke the kiss, and my mouth latched voraciously onto one of her taut nipples. My tongue swirled around its dark brown button, reveling in its unusual texture and the salty-sweet taste of her skin. The throaty sound of her voice moaning my name had even more blood rushing to my groin.

Too drunk with pleasure and desire, hungry for more of the divine power building in my chest—power I could feel myself sucking right out of my woman—I ignored the lancing pain steadily growing in my back.

With a boldness I'd never believed myself capable of, I slipped my hand under the waist of her skirt, inside her slip, and straight to her burning core. Esmeralda cried out my name, her back arching off the tree, involuntarily pressing her chest to my face as my tongue continued to lave her nipple.

Despite having never been with a female before, I wasn't clueless about a woman's anatomy or how to pleasure one. Perched at the top of the spire for two decades, I'd seen my fair share of naughty action in the streets of Paris, the woods surrounding the temple, and even in the temple gardens themselves, both days and nights.

But never would I have imagined the silky wetness that greeted me when my fingers explored Esmeralda's core. The sound of her labored breathing and sighs of pleasure, the way she shivered and gyrated her hips in response to my touch, her feverish hands on me, fisting my hair and clutching one of my horns, had me mad with lust.

On instinct, I accelerated the movement on my hand massaging the little nub at the apex of her legs. I could feel her begin to crest as her body trembled against mine, and her moans came in louder, shorter bursts. I covered her neck and face with kisses, sucking at her tender flesh, willing her to climax for me.

And then she did.

Lightning literally struck between us, electric tendrils writhing all over her body as she cried out in rapture. A massive bolt of power emanating from Esmeralda slammed into me. The blissful sensation reverberated directly in my groin, tearing an orgasm from me. But as I spilled my seed, relieving some of the strain on my cock still confined within my pants, my roar of ecstasy quickly shifted into one of agony.

I tore myself away from Esmeralda and stumbled a few steps back before falling to my knees. A constant stream of energy poured out of her and flowed into me. My body craved it, wanted more of it… wanted ALL of it. But my hump felt on the verge of bursting open. Palms resting on the ground, head hanging low, I gritted my teeth through the pain of searing hot blades stabbing at my spine.

"Kwazeem?" Esmeralda asked in a shaky voice filled with concern.

From the corner of my eye, I saw her fumble with her chest bandeau to cover herself while rushing to my side.

*No! No! Don't approach me.*

Which each step, the intensity of the power within grew and with it, the agony robbing me of coherent thoughts. Her warm palm settling on my shoulder in what should have been a comforting gesture felt like vicious claws slashing me to the bone. I cried out and instinctively batted her hand away with far more force than intended. She yelped and cradled her wrist to her chest. The debilitating pain in my back kept me from expressing the guilt and horror I felt at having physically hurt her in any way.

"You're doing this. Move away!" were the words that tumbled out of my mouth instead of the apology I'd intended. "Get away from me."

"But—"

"GO AWAY! LEAVE! I DON'T WANT YOU HERE!"

My vocal chords hurt having shouted so loud. Esmeralda's choked sob, followed by her quickly fading steps barely registered through the fog of misery that had engulfed me. Although the ball of power she'd fed into me had finally stopped growing with her departure, it pulsated strong and bright like a glowing sun in my chest. Each pulsating sensation renewed and enhanced the stabbing pain in my hump. Through blurred vision, I watched my hands swell at an exponential rate, and purplish blotches appear on my bluish-grey skin.

The last thing I saw before my eyelids swelled, forcing my eyes closed, was the worried face of Victus landing in front of me.

# CHAPTER 8
## ESMERALDA

I needed answers. And, more importantly, I needed to help Kwazeem. Things had started out so perfect before he went completely berserk on me.

I'd never felt more hurt and more rejected than in that instant. For the few hours that followed, I'd remained curled up on my bed, feeling dirty and lower than dirt, thinking he'd cast me aside for being too easy, or for having lost interest now that he'd gotten what he'd wanted. What a stupid reaction on my part. Clearly, Kwazeem had been in pain, but my mind had remained stuck on his words, ordering me to leave the minute I'd climaxed.

It took me far too long to get my head straight and see that situation for what it had been; his condition suddenly manifesting itself. Then again, I was feeling emotionally drained. Ellen's words replayed in my mind while I attempted to decide what to do. I'd been too lost first in pleasure and then in hurt to rationalize what had happened. Now, with my head clear, I remembered the way his hump appeared to grow and heave, stretching the shirt that had previously sat loosely across his shoulders. His hands, clutching the ground, had appeared swollen with patches of redness. But, through all that, and from the very moment Kwazeem had begun kissing me, a flow of energy had formed between us. No… not a flow. *My* energy had been flowing towards him.

And yet, just like in the chapel during my first Chant here, my power had felt enhanced, stronger than ever before. At the same time my Light had flown into him, his aura had fueled me, replenishing it in a continuous cycle of give and take. I couldn't dismiss Ellen's words that a Fallen would drain me of my Vestal power. But what had happened didn't align with what she said.

A quick look at the clock indicated it was already a little after two in the afternoon. Jumping out of bed, I splashed some water on my face and swiftly changed into clothes better suited for hiking. There was enough time for me to catch a shuttle to and from the Godswood before nightfall.

But first, I needed to check on Kwazeem.

More grateful than ever that there was no rehearsal today, and that both Frollo and the Light Maidens were absent, I snuck back to the hidden passage, keeping my power in check so that he couldn't sense my approach. Finding his house empty worried me. I hastened down the path to the river, stopping a far distance away as soon as I noticed his silhouette sitting on the ground by the tree, the remains of our picnic carefully tucked back into the basket. Although I couldn't clearly see from where I stood, Kwazeem appeared to be cradling the costume I had brought him to his chest. I couldn't tell if the pained expression on his face stemmed from his condition or from whatever thoughts tormented him. However, watching him pet his imps reassured me he wasn't in any physical distress.

For a moment, I considered approaching him again, but decided against it. I wasn't sure if he would welcome my presence just now, and I wouldn't know what to say. Turning on my heels, I made a beeline for the public transport hub at the edge of the open market. Naturally, I stood out in the crowd despite my common outfit. Vestals rarely traveled amidst the common folk, using instead the Chariot of Light or private transportation provided by the Praetor.

However, I didn't want to alert Frollo as to my whereabouts. Using either of the latter methods would have required a pilot taking me to my destination. While I had no intentions of hiding that visit from him, I couldn't risk him preemptively warning Old Nan against telling me anything. Instead, I rented a Tear—Vesta's Tear to be more precise. Shaped like a drop of water lying horizontally, Tears were private shuttles only big enough for two passengers and a small cargo at the back. It traveled great distances at high speed, purely relying on either solar or Vestal energy. Despite the disturbing name for a vehicle, Tears had proven themselves beyond safe even in heavily trafficked areas. Thanks to their advanced GPS system and autopilot ability, the small vessels could be dropped anywhere on the planet, and it could autopilot itself back to the closest Tear hangar.

No one would question me visiting Old Nan's Trading Post. In fact, it featured in the list of preset popular shopping destinations on the Tear's interface. I barely paid any attention to the beautiful landscape sprawling before me under the bright, early-afternoon sun. In the distance, the weak luminous beams of two spires marked the center of smaller cities surrounding Paris. In two days, after the Festival of Light, Frollo would visit each one to give them a recharged Orb—assuming I performed as expected.

*And he'd hope for you to tag along with him.*

That wouldn't happen. Even if nothing came of that thing between Kwazeem and me, I could never belong to Frollo. I barely knew the gardener, and yet something unique was binding us. I'd spent my life dreaming of the day I'd stand before an Elohim, hoping to find grace in his eyes. The day after tomorrow, I would meet the greatest of them all, High Seraph Phoebus, but I couldn't care less. A single male occupied my every thought.

As the autopilot landed my Tear in the small clearing surrounding Old Nan's Trading Post, I was relieved to see only three other vessels. With the Festival only a few hours away, most people were too busy scrambling with last minute preparations to be out shopping. But what struck me the most were the eerie similarities between the lines and shapes of this Trading Post and those of Kwazeem's house. Although not identical, Kwazeem had clearly been inspired by the home of his childhood.

The door of the Tear silently slid open, and I hopped out, my stomach fluttering with an odd mix of anticipation and worry. What if Nan didn't wish to speak to me or pretended she didn't know anything about Kwazeem? It suddenly dawned on me how impulsive I'd yet again behaved. What in the world was wrong with me? I'd always been the deliberate, organized, and rational one among my Vestal sisters. And now, I kept reacting based on whatever emotion stirred me the most. Considering how all over the place they'd been since setting foot on Eden, I should try harder to rein myself in.

*But I'm here now, and I need answers.*

Taking in a deep breath, I marched with determined steps towards the one story house. Built in length, with tall, reflective windows and flowery vines climbing some of its walls, the wooden structure had been cleverly designed to almost blend with the surrounding forest. As I walked up to the large set of doors, they swished open almost silently onto a modern shop that still managed to scream rustic and natural.

The sweet aroma of potpourri and scented candles greeted me. To my surprise, the front store wasn't crumbling under stacks of products or shopping baskets. Customers picked up a small data key at the entrance of the store and simply scanned the demonstrator of the products they wanted, with a small interface allowing them to indicate quantity. I picked up a key while casting furtive glances at the two women behind the counter.

A younger female in her late thirties was taking the keys from the customers and fetching their orders at the back. The older female, which I immediately knew to be Old Nan, took payments from the customer or haggled the trades that didn't involve credits. Trying not to draw more attention than necessary, I casually browsed the goods on offering, scanning quite a few of the jars of fruit jams for Kwazeem. Two of the five customers inside left, and I crossed my fingers that no new ones would come in before the remaining three departed.

I was looking at a series of stunning colorful fabrics the likes I'd never seen before when a painting on a nearby wall caught my eye. My breath caught in my throat as I took in the image of a gorgeous little boy with pale bluish skin. Sitting cross-legged by a creek, he stared in awe at the large egg in his hands from whence the head of a newborn imp, in the process of hatching, peeked out. I immediately knew it to be a lifelike representation of Kwazeem and Victus.

I don't know how long I stood there, transfixed by the realism and perfection of the image.

"Stunning boy, isn't he?" a soft voice said over my shoulder, startling me out of my dazed stupor.

I turned to find Old Nan standing near me, a gentle expression on her wizened face. I couldn't quite tell her origins judging by her thick, curly silver hair, tanned skin from frequent exposure to the sun, and her big, greenish-brown eyes that hinted at possible alien blood thrown into her human heritage.

"Breathtaking… Just like the man Kwazeem has grown into," I replied, my gaze holding hers unwaveringly.

She didn't flinch, recoil, or otherwise appear shocked. A knowing smile stretched her lips, and she gestured with her head for me to follow. Heart pounding, I followed in her wake under the curious stares of the remaining customer and the younger woman working behind the counter.

"Cover for me, Karolyn," Nan said. "I'll be at the house for a little while."

"Yes, Nan," Karolyn responded, her brown eyes burning with curiosity.

We exited the Trading Post through the back door, then walked in silence along a packed dirt path through the woods to a smaller house two hundred meters away. My jaw dropped at recognizing it as an exact replica of Kwazeem's house, while the Trading Post only shared many similarities.

"You recognized this house," Nan said, breaking the silence as she unlocked the door to her house.

"Yes," I admitted. "Kwazeem is currently building his new home identically to this one."

Nan smiled like a proud mother before waving me into the house. "Have a seat," she said, indicating the cushioned wooden chairs surrounding a massive, intricately carved redwood table. "I cannot grant you much time, but I would hear about my Kwazeem before answering a few of whatever questions you may have. Tea?"

I nodded absentmindedly, suddenly feeling as if she'd been waiting for me—or at least for some Vestal—to come see her about Kwazeem.

"Yes, I knew one of you would eventually come," Nan said. She chuckled when I gaped at her for reading my mind, but continued to put some water to boiling. "Don't be so surprised, child. Your face is very expressive. Many of your sisters have come through here over the years. Each time, I hoped they were coming to inquire about my boy. But every time, they were merely here to browse my products. You, however… The minute you walked in, I knew that the day had come at last."

Nan brought two cups and some berry breads to the table,

while the water was quickly heating. I opened my mouth to offer to help, but she didn't give me a chance.

"Do you love him?" she asked.

My heart leaped in my chest, and I squirmed in my chair, unsure how to answer.

"I… I barely know him," I said cautiously.

"But?" she insisted before pouring the boiling water into a teapot.

"But I am very drawn to him, and he to me," I conceded. "However, I am a very public figure, and—"

"And the mob will descend upon him for defiling an Anointed," Nan interrupted, her voice hardening slightly. "Tell me child, does he drain you?"

I hesitated, unsure how to answer truthfully. "Until today, no. And even today, not really. Or at least, I'm not sure what to make of it. Before, his presence always only enhanced my power, and I mean *significantly* enhanced it. But this morning, I felt as if he was absorbing my Light, but also replenishing it. I only felt emotionally drained, not physically, and not my power," I quickly added, feeling the need to protect him somehow.

Nan smiled, making my cheeks heat.

"Even without the townsfolk opposing any potential relationship between Kwazeem and me, I fear our natures might not be compatible," I said, hoping she would be able to shed some light on some of the questions haunting me. "Ellen, one of the open market merchants, said a Fallen will permanently drain a Vestal of her powers. Is this what is happening with Kwazeem?"

Nan took a moment to reflect on her answer, choosing her words carefully as she poured us both a cup of tea.

"It is true that, since the Fall, the Light Bearers involuntarily drain the Vestals of their Divine Light when exposed long enough to them," the older lady said, settling at the table across from me. She held the steamy cup of tea in her hands as if to warm them, her gaze lingering on the amber liquid it contained.

"But Kwazeem isn't a pureblood Fallen. He's special. His mother had to live isolated from her tribe because the other Fallen were passively harming the child."

"Passively?" I asked, confused.

"The same way humans cannot tolerate extended exposure to an Elohim's aura before starting to manifest symptoms similar to radiation poisoning, the Fallen's aura threatened to kill Kwazeem," Nan said before taking a sip of her tea, her eyes staring blindly in the distance as she reminisced. "Which each passing month of her pregnancy, the farther she had to be from her people. When the time came to deliver, she was alone. With complications kicking in, she called her clan, but they couldn't approach without killing the child. So, one of her clanmates named Mikku came to ask me for help. But I arrived there too late." Nan refocused on me, a sad look on her face. "She was so young and so beautiful… She died minutes after naming her son and making me promise to look after him."

My throat tightened at imagining the terrified young woman trying to bring a new life into this world, all by herself. And, worse still, handing the child she would never get to see grow into a man off to a complete stranger.

"I don't understand. Why did she stay with the tribe?" I asked. "Even if she'd been shunned for consorting with a Fallen, and despite losing her powers, she was still a Vestal. By law, the doctors in Paris would have been obligated to assist her and the baby."

"She wasn't a Vestal," Nan deadpanned before taking another sip of her tea.

I gaped at her, totally taken aback by that statement. Considering the strong power I felt within Kwazeem, I'd naturally assumed his mother had been a high-ranking Vestal.

"Kwazeem's mother was a Fallen name Caleeza," Nan continued. "She never would have been allowed close enough to the city to receive treatment. And bringing a doctor here would have probably gotten us both in trouble." Nan sighed heavily and ran a hand through her silver mane. "I don't know who his father was, but he must have been a powerful ergokinetic. Caleeza said he must have died or he would have returned to her and their unborn child."

*Would he?*

Nan chuckled, and my cheeks heated as my expressive face had no doubt given away my thoughts.

"I've wondered, too," Nan admitted. "He wouldn't have been the first man to have tried to 'score' a Fallen female. But I fear we'll never know. I love the boy as my own. He was such a good kid. So full of energy, but always affectionate and obedient. When his condition first manifested, I thought we would manage. He'd been so great adapting to his hump, not letting it interfere with his day-to-day life. And then it got worse, and worse, and even worse."

Nan let out a shuddering breath, her gaze haunted by the souvenir of helplessly watching 'her child' in agony. I instinctively reached out and grabbed her hand in a comforting gesture. Her fingers tightened around it, and she gave me a shaky smile of gratitude.

"I was so desperate I went to a Fallen village and barely got away with my life. But Mikku, the male who had come to ask me to help Caleeza, remembered me," Nan continued. "He accepted my request to come see her son, but once more, Kwazeem went into seizures when Mikku came too close. The blood samples I gave him to analyze revealed nothing helpful. I was preparing mentally for my boy to die, dosing him with poppy milk in the hopes of easing his remaining days. And then Frollo showed up at my shop."

I straightened in my chair, listening with anticipation at what might provide me with the answers I sought.

"He had come in like any other customer, although he'd been particularly interested in medicinal herbs and meditation oils and candles," Nan said, an odd expression on her face. "Moments after he entered, he started looking around with a confused look, as if searching for something, although he mostly stared at the back of the store. I eventually asked him what was wrong, and he asked if there was a Vestal in here."

"A Vestal?" I asked, taken aback by the odd question.

"I'd been as surprised as you are," Nan said with a sympathetic smile. "But then I nearly panicked when he said there was a powerful ergokinetic nearby. He could feel their energy. Naturally, I denied it, until he dropped the subject. The next few days were terrifying. Not only was Kwazeem's condition becoming critical, but Frollo kept coming back, his gaze full of suspicion."

"Did he challenge you each time he came?"

"No, he just came in, pretended to look at the products on offering, while lurking around to assess where the energy emanated from," Nan said, shaking her head. "That day, he left as usual without a fuss. A few hours after the shop had closed, I took Kwazeem to the river to try and break his fever."

"And Frollo showed up," I said, guessing where the story was headed.

Nan nodded. "Yes. He admitted afterwards that he'd been hiding in the shadows, fearing I might be holding a Vestal or a gifted child against their will and in contravention with the laws."

*No way...*

I didn't believe for one minute that righteous zeal had dictated his actions.

"But whatever his reasons, he immediately took an interest in Kwazeem. And instead of reporting me to the authorities, he offered to help." Her hand tightened further around mine. "He was the miracle I'd been praying for; the miracle that would save my boy's life. And he did. I didn't understand the medical jargon he laid on me regarding Kwazeem's condition. I didn't really care either beyond the fact that my boy was no longer in agony.

But then, it kept coming back. In the meantime, Frollo had been climbing the ranks at dizzying speed to become the youngest Praetor in our history. That's when he asked to take Kwazeem from me to go live in Paris with him."

"But why?" I asked, happy to finally get to the part Kwazeem hadn't been able to tell me much about. "Why take him to a place that could get them both executed for breaking the law? Why not just keep coming here once a month to care for him?"

"Those are the very questions I asked him," Nan said, a frown marring her forehead. "I didn't want to part with my baby, but with his new duties, Frollo couldn't justify his escapades anymore. The way his schedule was tightly managed, with his personal guards almost always by his side, it would rapidly raise suspicions. That hadn't fully convinced me, but then Frollo said he'd been building a lab in the temple where he could spend all of his free time looking for a cure if Kwazeem was nearby."

"So, you let him go," I said softly, wondering if I could have done it.

"I often wondered if it had been a mistake," Nan said. "But I couldn't risk Frollo abandoning my baby if I refused."

"I still don't understand why Frollo would put his life and career on the line for a Fallen half-breed," I insisted.

"I asked him that very question," Nan said, making me perk up. "He said that a being who possessed Divine Light couldn't be evil. As Praetor and Guardian of Vesta's Temple on the First Circle, it was his duty to protect all of her children, whatever their genetics."

"With all due respect, that sounds like a whole lot of hot air to me," I said, frustrated.

Nan burst out laughing. "That was my thought, too, but beggars can't be choosers. For all that, Frollo has kept his promises except about keeping me informed about my boy's welfare. He was diligent about it in the first couple of years, but as time went by, I heard less and less frequently, and now not at all. For a while, I would come to the Chakra ceremonies in the hopes of catching a glimpse of Kwazeem, but he was kept too well hidden. So, your presence is a balm on my old heart to know my baby still thrives."

"He is thriving, despite his condition still plaguing him, but they have a routine now so that he can function normally," I said, leaving out the way it had been escalating lately. "He's a fantastic gardener and weapons smith. And his two imps, Victus and Lazarus, are a riot. They love to hug and kiss people. Kwazeem is always scolding them so that they leave me alone."

"Not people," Nan gently corrected. "They only show such affection to people they recognize as kindred spirits. They hug you because they love you."

My face heated with embarrassment and pleasure. But I quickly sobered before asking the question that had been burning my tongue for days.

"Is there any chance Frollo could be blood-related to Kwazeem?"

Nan slightly recoiled, taken aback by a question she'd clearly never even contemplated. "No. Why do you ask?"

"Since he would have been in his early teens when Kwazeem was conceived, I doubt he's the father," I explained, making a slight detour before getting to my point. "But he could be his older brother. Frollo's ergokinetic powers are impressive for a human male. I thought he'd inherited it from his mother, whom I'd assumed had been a high-ranking Vestal. You see, Frollo's Divine Light is almost identical to Kwazeem's. That's impossible unless they are related. Frankly, I'd only ever felt something so similar between twins, and even then... That would also explain why Frollo has been so steadfast in looking after him."

"I see what you mean, but it is not possible. Frollo's father was a struggling merchant from Loriend, a small town in the suburbs of Paris. He died of liver failure after years of heavy drinking when Frollo was still a boy. Even the mechanical implant they'd given him as a replacement couldn't handle his continued alcohol abuse."

"Does Frollo have a brother or an uncle?" I asked, running out of options.

Nan shook her head with a commiserating look. "Unfortunately, no. It warms my heart that Kwazeem should have someone such as you in his life, someone who clearly cares about him. But I caution you to tread carefully and understand well the consequences of your choices. A life with him could mean the loss of your Divine Light and the end of your life as a Vestal. You will live in exile as the people aren't ready to accept a Fallen in their midst. Kwazeem might even be hunted for 'defiling' an Anointed."

I flinched at the truth of her words, the dark side that I wasn't ready to handle just yet.

"Your arrival on Eden has brought great hope to our people. No Vestal has come even remotely close to filling our Well. And with our cities constantly expanding, the energy supply no longer meets the demand," Nan explained, a troubled look on her face. "Every Vestal who has come to Paris ended up fleeing to lesser Circles, burnt out and exhausted from endless demands for more energy. People said the beacon of the temple's spire glowed like a high noon sun when you performed your first Chant, such was the power of your Divine Light. Now, all our hopes rest on you. There will be a record attendance the day after tomorrow for your first Festival. If Kwazeem robs you of your Light, the citizens will descend upon him like a rabid mob."

I refused to even contemplate the possibility of losing my power. It didn't define me, but it was an integral part of me. I had devoted my life to becoming the light bringer of the people. As an Anointed, I'd been blessed with more power than most Vestals would ever yield in their lifetime. Such a gift came with great responsibilities. How could I even contemplate throwing this all away over my intense attraction to Kwazeem?

"One last thing to keep in mind," Nan continued, her voice gentle despite the clear warning it contained. "Kwazeem is only still alive thanks to the Praetor's ministrations. Before you even contemplate running away together, make sure you can aid him in a similar fashion. My boy has already suffered far too much."

My chest constricted at the thought of so many hurdles before us.

"Your words have not fallen into deaf ears," I whispered, feeling somewhat defeated.

The hard glint that had crept into Nan's eyes faded, replaced by sympathy and a sliver of guilt. "I would love nothing more than for you two to find a way to make it work. But I want even more for my boy to live and to remain safe. His life may be empty, and quite lonely at times, but it's a decent one. Please, make sure you do not make it worse."

# CHAPTER 9
### KWAZEEM

I trudged towards the plaza with steps as heavy as my heart, my hovercart laden with bioluminescent flowers and my two imps in tow. The way I'd yelled at Esmeralda to go away replayed in an infernal loop in my mind. The hurt and humiliated look in her eyes as she fixed her clothes and ran away was forever burned in my psyche. She had completely misunderstood my reaction, but how could she not?

The lancing pain in my back had remained my constant companion since yesterday morning; since Esmeralda had so greatly honored me by surrendering herself to my touch. Strong emotions—mainly joy—seemed to cause Esmeralda to project her Divine Light, creating a power link between us. But as much as it gave me pleasure, it would eventually kill me. A quick look in the mirror last night had confirmed what my blotchy, swollen hands and the throbbing in my face had heralded. It had only been four days since Frollo had last drained me. And yet, my face already looked as disfigured as if I'd been at the start of the last week of my condition's monthly cycle.

I blinked away the tears pricking my eyes at this reminder that I could never be with the one woman to have touched my heart. How arrogant to have ever even contemplated it? Of course, her Divine Light would repel one as unworthy as I. Esmeralda needed to know I'd only asked her to leave because her presence was crippling me. With Frollo out of town until the next day, had my condition worsened, I would have been a wreck for twenty-four hours, with no one to save me. I hated being so dependent, so helpless.

After I'd gotten my pain under control late yesterday afternoon, I'd snuck into the temple to explain and apologize, but Esmeralda had been gone. Today, with the frantic activity surrounding the last-minute preparations for the Festival tomorrow, there had been no opportunities to approach her. Even sending my imps with a note would have been too risky.

I placed my portable hovering platform by the wall of the tall building surrounding the plaza. Stepping onto it, I rose a few meters above ground to adorn the façade with bioluminescent flowers. Their dreamy glow in the darkness of night, only otherwise bathed by the pale moon, soothed some of my sorrow. Victus and Lazarus brought me more flowers from my hovercart as I decorated the nearby buildings and the Elohim perches by the Well of Power.

I was heading towards the table of honor when the light in Esmeralda's room turned on. My heart skipped a beat when, moments later, her slender silhouette appeared at her balcony. With my hawkish eyesight, I watched her looking for me in the darkness. Even with the moonlight, humans couldn't clearly see me unless I stood under a brighter light.

Raising my hovering platform near one of the walls illuminated by the flowers, I stopped where she would have the greatest chance of seeing me. Her eyes widened when she found me at last. Hesitant at first, she smiled and waved timidly at me. My chest constricted with emotion realizing that, despite my horrible behavior, she appeared not to hold a grudge. Raising my hand in the light, I waved back. Her smile broadened, and she slightly bowed her head before returning back inside.

But even as darkness swallowed her room again, my silly grin persisted through the pain. With renewed energy, and an inexplicable sense of hope, I went back to work, counting the hours until the Festival.

"How the fuck did your condition progress so quickly?" Frollo demanded, eyeing me with a mix of suspicion and confusion.

As with every Festival of Light, he always brought me a basket of food with minced pies, pastries, roasted meats and sautéed vegetables. Those were the best meals I ever got to enjoy, even though they weren't as good as I imagined the ones fresh out of the oven tasted on the plaza. I never quite understood this odd kindness Frollo showed me on those occasions—not that he was ever actually cruel to me.

"I don't know," I said with partial honesty as I genuinely didn't understand why Esmeralda's power affected me in such a way when other Vestals never had. "But I will need to be drained in the next few days again."

I gave him an apologetic look for being such a burden to him. What I wouldn't give to be able to perform the procedure on my own.

"Right…" Frollo said pensively.

The absence of annoyance in his demeanor made me feel better. For all my misgivings about the Praetor, he'd never balked or complained about helping me with my condition. Well, except for that night I'd intruded on Esmeralda's Chant. Cupping my face in his hands, he tilted my head left then right while examining my swollen features.

"I will be performing the Orb Relay to the peripheral city

tonight and tomorrow after the Festival. When I return on Sunday, we'll assess your condition," Frollo said before releasing me.

"Thank you," I said with genuine gratitude. The pain was still tolerable, but not for long. And draining my spine too frequently could do permanent damage. So, we had to delay as much as possible.

Frollo harrumphed his acknowledgment as he always did whenever I thanked him for any act of kindness, as if it embarrassed him or made him uncomfortable. Turning around, he headed for the door to my cabin, then appeared to hesitate. He looked at me over his shoulder, a frown on his forehead as if he debated with himself.

"Once the celebrations begin, you may watch from the spire. But see that you return here before the festivities end."

I gaped at him, stunned by that unexpected about face. He'd been so furious with me for sneaking into the chapel. My mouth opened and closed, words failing me, but Frollo didn't wait for my answer. I watched his receding back, feeling more confused than ever. Victus and Lazarus pawing restlessly at the food basket Frollo had brought forced me to refocus. I opened it and gave them small pieces of meat to chew on. Munching absentmindedly on a slice of minced pie, my feet led me to my bedroom and to the closet where I'd hidden the Fallen mask Esmeralda had brought me.

For the past couple of days, I'd gone back and forth in my mind whether to use it. Until a few moments ago, I'd intended to do so in order not to miss out on the celebration completely. But now that I could return to my old quarters, even if only for a few hours, did it make sense to put myself and Frollo at risk by traipsing the streets of Paris amidst the crowd?

*But I want to...*

I *badly* wanted to. For once, I would belong, surrounded by all the other citizens, dancing, laughing, and singing with them.

No one would question or challenge my presence. With my costume, I would blend into the crowd.

*But what if my condition acts up again?*

I could rush back to the temple the minute the symptoms manifested themselves… or rather, if they noticeably increased since pain already plagued me. As long as I didn't go too far down the plaza, it would be no problem. And with all eyes focused on Esmeralda, the Well of Power, and the Elohim, no one would notice my discreet exit.

Silencing the unease swirling in the pit of my stomach, I spent the next couple of hours rationalizing all the ways this made sense. I'd never had such a perfect costume before, and I could help Esmeralda. She'd been nervous about her performance, knowing what high expectations everyone had of her. But my presence enhanced her power. Even if I needed to run halfway through my woman's dance, she would blow away everyone's mind.

As the first notes of music rose over the city, I stood in front of my mirror with my Fallen mask over my head, the holographic suit reinforcing my alien appearance, and the cloak for good measure. The mask had much bigger horns on the forehead than my own, and thicker scales over a larger surface of my cheeks. Instead of the mostly discreet facial spikes along my jawline, the mask had a series of bone spikes ending on each side of my chin. The mask didn't cover my mouth. Normally, bluish-grey makeup would have been used to match my skin to it, but it was unnecessary for me. The holographic suit gave my hands long, hooked claws, far more vicious looking than my own when I extruded them.

Heart pounding, I made my way to one of the secret back entrances into the temple, then used the lift to go up to the spire. Entering my old room, I made my way to the balcony to assess the situation outside. Frollo was already standing on the dais where the table of honor had been erected, speaking with some dignitaries from the peripheral cities. As expected, Esmeralda and the Light Maidens were nowhere to be seen. They would make a grand entrance in thirty minutes or so, when the trumpets would herald the impending arrival of the Elohim.

An already thick crowd milled about, cheering on the public entertainers performing over the reinforced glass plate covering the Well. Many a bystander flocked from one of the large buffet tables to the next where generous helpings of various amuse-bouche had been laid out for all to freely indulge in. Once the Ceremony of Light to charge the Well of Power ended, a feast would replace these appetizers.

Unable to resist, I gave in to the wish that had been denied to me for the past two decades, since my first arrival in Paris as a child. Despite the burning urge to finally exit the temple through the main doors, I snuck out onto the plaza from one of the open gates into the garden. No one would question a reveler traipsing about the temple's backyard, which I always specially decorated for the Festival.

I could barely breathe from my heart pounding so frantically into my throat. Walking on shaky legs, I threaded my way through the throngs. My head spun from having so many people around me, but in a good way; in a happily drunken way. The energy amongst the crowd was overcharged.

None of them knew me, and yet they smiled at me and laughed *with* me. Many complimented me for my fabulous costume. A pretty female I'd often seen working at one of the stalls of the open market grabbed both my hands and spun us around three times. Disoriented, I gaped at the woman when she smacked a loud kiss on my cheek, released my hands, and waved goodbye with a beaming smile. Seconds later, she hooked arms with another female and they spun around, too, before parting ways to a different partner.

I burst out laughing, feeling free, feeling happy… feeling like I belonged.

Losing all inhibitions, I stopped trying to walk straighter. No one questioned my stooped posture as I, too, went from table to table to sample the food offering. Even though the amuse-bouche were the same as the assortment Frollo had brought me, food had never tasted so divine than in that instant.

Overwhelmed by this emotional and sensory overload, I didn't see time fly. The blaring trumpets snapped me out of my unbridled revelry. A hush fell over the crowd that suddenly sobered. Like a neatly sliced ripe fruit, the people parted with almost military discipline on each side of the plaza. The main doors of the temple opened on Esmeralda in the lead, followed by ten Light Maidens, paired in twos.

It shocked me to realize how far I'd gotten from the temple, carried away by the celebrating crowd. But that didn't matter. The breathtaking sight of the Anointed Vestal had everyone entranced. Dressed in a shimmering neck wrap crop top, embroidered with glow pearls, and a short sarong skirt in a similar pale fabric, Esmeralda seemed to glide rather than walk as she approached the plaza.

The glass dome covering the Well of Power parted. The five rings of the Well, each of them flat, indicated the five main peripheral cities of Paris, which supplied energy for the sprawling suburbs surrounding them. In the center of the Well, a spire-like tower rose barely a meter above ground. That sight further sobered the crowd. The energy reserves had never been so low. The ancient glyphs on both the tower and the rings pulsated in an alarmingly weak fashion.

Esmeralda stopped in front of the well—although not stepping onto it—and faced the table of honor. The Light Maidens formed a line on each side of her, all facing the dais as well. But they weren't looking at Frollo or the dignitaries who had all risen to their feet. Heads tilted upwards, they gazed upon the majestic Elohim flying down from their floating city, Elysium. There was something hypnotic to the rhythmic way the wide span of their wings flapped around them. The setting sun reflecting just the right way on their gleaming armor further enhanced that impression by giving them an almost angelic halo.

The crowd all but held its breath as twenty of the giant winged warriors settled on the perches erected around the plaza for them, the sound of their wings ominous. Only the three Seraphs landed by the dais: High Seraph Phoebus, and the two generals of his legions, Arrius and Magnus. Unlike the white-winged Elohim perched around the plaza—Angels, Archangels and Dominions—the three Seraphs had a double set of black wings with white spotted down feathers on the top set around their shoulders. It could have almost passed for a king's ermine fur.

Even from where we stood, their aura could be felt, drawing you in like the most irresistible addiction, and instilling fear of the harm extended exposure would cause to the common human. Despite their obvious urge to come closer, the people of Paris moved farther back from the Well and the divine guests surrounding it.

Once more, a pang of envy coursed through me at the perfection of the Elohim. Over seven feet tall, with heavenly faces and glowing eyes, their godly, muscular bodies were bare but for the adorned leather skirts and gladiator sandals they wore. However, while the audience—especially the females—couldn't tear their gazes away from them, the Elohim only had eyes for one woman —MY woman.

A burning jealousy rose from the darkest depths of me when Phoebus placed his palm over his heart and bowed his head at Esmeralda with a seductive smile. The glyph on the armband adorning his wrist flashed, something I'd never seen in all the past years when he'd greeted the Vestal serving at the time. My Mera placed both hands over her own heart and bowed her head, imitated seconds later by the Light Maidens.

As soon as the women straightened, Frollo approached the Elohim leader and his generals.

"Welcome to Paris, High Seraph Phoebus, and honorable Generals Arrius and Magnus. You honor us with your presence."

Despite the distance, my enhanced eyesight and hearing allowed me to see and hear all that the rest of the people in attendance could only speculate about.

"The honor is all ours, Praetor," Phoebus said with his thundering voice, although his gaze never strayed from Esmeralda. "We wouldn't have missed the opportunity to meet an Anointed."

I didn't miss Frollo slightly clenching his jaw in displeasure, a sentiment I shared all too well. What male could rival a Seraph? Esmeralda *was* an Anointed, born to walk at the side of a god. What chance could a deformed creature such as I possibly stand against so many better males?

"I am certain she will be just as delighted to make your acquaintance after the ceremony," Frollo responded with an award-winning performance of cordiality. "If you please," he added, gesturing to the table of honor.

Tearing his gaze away from Esmeralda with visible effort, Phoebus finally made eye contact with Frollo. He frowned before giving the Praetor an assessing look.

"Your power has grown again, and significantly, too, since the last time we've met," Phoebus said in a confused voice. "Your Light is verging the divine. It calls to me like that of a brother. And yet, I know of no Vestals in your bloodline."

Frollo puffed his chest, failing miserably to hide his pride. "You flatter me, High Seraph. But I must admit that Esmeralda has awakened within me things I didn't know existed. Having her by my side has enhanced me in ways I never imagined possible."

As much as I wanted to punch him in the throat for his obvious innuendos, it hurt me that she would impact the Praetor the same way she had me. It was stupid but, for some silly reason, I'd convinced myself that a special bond that existed *only* between the two of us had enhanced Esmeralda's powers and awakened the one inside me.

Phoebus narrowed his gaze at Frollo, having clearly understood the underlying message. "You shouldn't be so surprised," the Seraph said dismissively. "Anointed Vestals are born to be the consorts of the gods. If they can enhance us, they would obviously affect common men."

That, too, struck a nerve. Under different circumstances, I would have been amused to see Frollo so righteously put back in his place. But the High Seraph's words rang with an undeniable truth that applied even more so to me.

Without waiting for Frollo's response, Phoebus marched to the central chair at the table of honor. Following in silence, the Praetor settled at his right, and the Seraph generals took a seat on either side of them. After bowing to the Seraphs, the five dignitaries of each of the main peripheral cities walked down the dais carrying with reverence a highly ornate round container the size of a giant pumpkin. In turn, they each stopped in front of Esmeralda before opening the container.

It revealed the Relay Orb of their respective cities. My woman held her palms on the side of the Orb without touching it and pushed her power inside it, causing a brief, stabbing pain at the base of my hump. The Orb immediately lit up and began to hover with a soft hum above the open container in the dignitary's hands. Two Light Maidens, one on each side of Esmeralda, approached and placed a hand on the side of the Orb, once more without touching it. Then, moving in coordinated steps, the Maidens went to take position at one of the five 'corners' of the Well with their Orb.

As each of the four remaining dignitaries repeated the process, the stabbing pain of Esmeralda activating their Orbs reminded me of my precarious situation. Soon she would begin her Chant to Vesta, and then her dance to invoke lightning and the power of her Divine Light to charge the Well and the Orbs. I had brought earplugs to block out her Chant, figuring the first half of her dance wouldn't harm me. But I hadn't expected her power to manifest so soon with such strength.

Trying to weave my way through the tightly packed crowd, panic began to settle in the pit of my stomach at my frighteningly slow progress. People were glaring at me, pushing back, annoyed at me interrupting their enjoyment of this sacred proceeding. They didn't understand where I was headed, and why I would even want to leave.

Despite the earplugs, the first crystalline note that rose from Esmeralda's throat pierced right through me down to my very core. Pleasure and pain flooded through my body as a blissful ball of power burst within me. As the Vestal's Chant continued to rise, the Light Maidens joined their voices to hers, and the magical link which brought me both ecstasy and misery formed between my woman and me.

I swallowed down a pained cry, becoming more forceful in my attempts to break through the crowd. They pushed back with increasing violence, angered that I would ruin the trance in which the Chant was putting them under. Esmeralda's ergokinetic aura exploded in a magnetic wave that had the assembled citizens gasp as one voice. The same awed and disbelieving looks marked every visage in the writhing mass of nameless men and women standing between me and my refuge as lightning struck the tower of the Well, and the first ring lit up.

But for me, it was a roar of agony that escaped my lips as the surge of power made me feel as if my spine was torn right out of my back. The crowd, finally understanding something was seriously amiss, began to part before me. I stumbled ahead half-blind by the swelling of my eyes and face. The mask on my head now felt too tight, squeezing my throbbing face from all sides.

As another mesmerized cry rose from the sea of humans in

which I drowned, my knees buckled at the torment tearing me asunder. Grunting and moaning, I half-crawled towards a destination now beyond my strength to reach.

The beating of drums announced the beginning of Esmeralda's dance. How I had wished to see it. How I had wished to be normal, once... just once. And now, I would die, a few meters from my beloved because I had been too bold, too reckless... Because I'd lusted after the consort of the gods.

# CHAPTER 10
## ESMERALDA

The very heart of Vesta beat through my chest as incommensurable power flowed through me. I was the alpha and the omega, the beginning and the end, the embodiment of Divine Light made flesh. I didn't need to see Kwazeem in the crowd to know this insane surge of power stemmed from him. He was both in and around me, lifting me to unparalleled heights.

The power of the Seraphs swirled around me, enhancing me further. They were battling each other for dominance, to claim me as their own. Phoebus's presence alone crushed any would-be competitor. And yet, his valiant efforts to form a link between us crashed repeatedly against the formidable bond that already existed between Kwazeem and me. But even the High Seraph's divine aura failed to rival how my Light responded to my Fallen. Whatever doubt might have lingered in my mind that Kwazeem and I were the two halves of the same whole vanished in that instant.

Lightning coursed through my body. Its sizzling coils spiraled around my bare arms and legs, and sparked at my fingertips. I acted as a conduit, absorbing the energy from the air, the elements, the ebullient crowd, and the divine aura of the Elohim, before transferring it into the Well. It greedily took all that I offered, its rings lighting up at dizzying speed. Even the Orbs hovering about the Maidens' hands crackled with energy.

Just as my power was reaching its apogee, a horrendous tearing pain sliced through my chest and my bond with Kwazeem was severed. I cried out, and lightning struck me dead center in the chest, at the same place the pain had originated. Arms wide spread, head thrown back, my body froze halfway through the swirl I'd been performing. Electric tendrils shot out from my hands, each beam connecting to the closest hovering Relay Orb on either side of me, then moving to the next until the Orbs and I were connected with a single continuous beam. The tower in the center of the Well grew taller by a couple of meters before shooting out a blinding ray of light into the early night sky.

The people roared their approval, a celebratory chant rising through their ranks.

The beam shooting out of my hands stopped abruptly, and I collapsed to my knees, head bowed and palms flat on the glowing surface of the Well. Although the sharp pain in my chest had faded, a hollowness persisted where my link with Kwazeem had connected us. Despite the loud ruckus of the overexcited citizens, the strong flapping sound of large wings reached me moments before the muscular arms of High Seraph Phoebus closed around me.

His aura slamming into me felt like a shot of adrenaline. With my connection to Kwazeem severed, Phoebus's Light poured into me with the violence of a river racing through a broken dam. A part of me hungered to embrace its purity and let myself become infused with his divinity. But Kwazeem's face flashed before my eyes, and I closed myself to the High Seraph, feeling as if basking in his aura would be like cheating on the one who had captured my heart.

Phoebus lifted me up, cradling me in his arms, a slight frown marring his angelic face. He once more attempted to pour his Light in to me, but I gently repelled it. It was unnecessary as his aura had already restored me from that moment of weakness.

"I've got you," Phoebus said, holding me like a bride.

I was opening my mouth to say he could put me down, when I noticed Frollo, looking furious, gesturing at his personal guards to go take care of something. Following the direction of his signal, I realized some sort of commotion was happening amidst the audience a couple of hundred meters from the temple.

"What's going on?" Phoebus asked Frollo.

Before he even answered, my stomach dropped to my feet, instinctively guessing what was coming next.

"Nothing important," Frollo said through clenched teeth. "Just one of my staff abusing my kindness. My guards will handle it. But please, do not let this distract us from this historical performance by our Anointed," he added with a forced smile, gesturing for us to head towards the table of honor.

"I... I can stand," I said to Phoebus, my palm tingling from the divine aura seeping into my palm resting on his bare chest.

"Are you certain?" Phoebus asked, making no mystery of his reluctance.

My face heated as I nodded timidly. "Yes, thank you. Your aura has done wonders for me."

He grunted his assent and, taking his sweet time, the High Seraph put me down, although his hand remained on my hip. Frollo's eyes flicked down to look at the possessive way Phoebus held me, and his expression further darkened. While the Praetor's feeling about it left me indifferent, I didn't want to send the wrong signal to the Seraph.

Advancing nonchalantly by a couple of steps, I 'accidentally' moved out of his grasp and then raised a hand to wave at the crowd that cheered me and the Maidens. This should have been a moment of complete triumph, but my gaze remained glued to the guards quickly approaching the location where a cluster of people had parted, forming a small circle around whatever—whoever—had caused that commotion.

I barely noticed the five dignitaries reclaiming their fully charged Relay Orbs from the Maidens. The guards, each hooking one arm under one of Kwazeem's, dragged him to the temple's garden entrance under the mocking jeers of the crowd who no doubt assumed he'd overindulged in alcohol. Knowing how proud he was, that his body remained limp made me fear the worst. Guilt gnawed at me for having incited him to leave the safety of the temple's grounds by giving him that costume. But I hated that he was essentially caged, wasting away at the edge of life, isolated and deprived of the most basic companionship, aside from his imps.

Phoebus's burning hand on the bare skin of the small of my back snapped me out of my troubled musings. With a last bow to the crowd still cheering us on, I let the High Seraph guide me to the table of honor. Sitting between Phoebus and Frollo, I spent the next couple of hours putting up with both of their shameless efforts at courting me. Each of the other Elohim flying down from their perches to introduce themselves to me and gauge my potential interest in them gave me a semblance of reprieve. To think I had spent years dreaming of the day I would be honored to receive the undivided attention of an Elohim.

But a single thought overwhelmed me: how was Kwazeem?

An orgy of food continued to be served to us in endless waves under the glowing light of the Well. I picked at my plate, half-listening to my companions and giving one or two-word answers to the questions that actually registered in my distracted mind. Frollo relentlessly attempted to entice me into joining him on the tour of the peripheral cities for the Relay Orb ceremonies by hyping their beauty. In direct contrast, Phoebus seemed to gracefully concede defeat. Although he, too, praised the virtues of life on Elysium, it was factual and anecdotal, the same way a charismatic tour guide delivered his speech. I genuinely liked the High Seraph. If not for Kwazeem, he could have easily swept me off my feet.

As the feast slowly neared its end, the rings of the Well of Power receded back into the ground, and the reinforced glass cover closed over it. Only the narrow tower at its center and its beam of light remained erect, the glass cover fitting snugly around it. The tower would gradually lower into the ground as the city's energy reserves started depleting, signaling the need for a new Festival.

"You have performed above and beyond all expectations," Phoebus said, abruptly changing the subject. "I have never met a Vestal as powerful as you, Esmeralda."

Blushing, my heart filling with pride, I lowered my gaze demurely. "Thank you, High Seraph. You flatter me."

"It is not flattery, merely facts," Phoebus replied with a shrug. "It has been years since anyone managed to fill the Well completely. You achieved that with a single Chant and a single dance. The only other time such an occurrence has been recorded was over a century ago, when the previous High Seraph Galleus and his Anointed consort, the Vestal Armina, presided over the Festival of Light. His bond to her enhanced her power a thousandfold. I had wished to claim a similar honor tonight, but I couldn't link with you. So, how did you achieve such godly levels?"

My heart skipped a beat. I couldn't tell him about Kwazeem doing for me what Galleus had done for his mate.

"Her power has grown since her arrival in Paris," Frollo intervened, sparing me from answering. "Just like mine. As I mentioned to you earlier, High Seraph, she has steadily been enhancing me."

The Praetor let the words hang between us, his implied meaning loud and clear for all. Under different circumstances, I'd have swiftly set the record straight. However, this served as a good enough explanation which also let me off the hook. I wanted to believe his interference had not just been motivated by self-preservation or possessiveness towards me, but out of protectiveness for Kwazeem. I still didn't fully understand the dynamic between them, but a part of me wanted to believe he cared.

*But then why has he still not gone to check on him?*

"I see," Phoebus said, his wings shifting with what I assumed to be annoyance. "I wanted to tempt you into letting me give you a personal tour of Elysium after the feast. Should I understand that such an offer would not be positively received due to prior engagements?"

His meaningful glance towards Frollo spoke volumes. I licked my lips nervously and shifted uncomfortably in my chair.

"No one in their right mind would refuse a guided tour of Elysium, especially one given by the High Seraph himself," I said, carefully choosing my words.

"But?" Phoebus insisted, his glowing eyes narrowing ever so slightly.

I smiled and tucked a strand of my long, curly hair behind my ear. "But, I would humbly request a different time than tonight. Praetor Frollo will shortly depart for his tour of the peripheral cities for the Orb Ceremonies. Once he does, I was hoping to call it an early night. This week, preparing for the Festival has been intense and, despite the regenerative effects of your aura, tonight's performance has drained me," I said with an apologetic expression.

Phoebus's expression softened, laced with a tinge of guilt. "Of course," he said, bowing his head slightly. "How insensitive of me not to have anticipated it. Your performance has so mesmerized all of us, we've stopped thinking clearly. I will escort you back to the temple right away, if you wish."

"Oh, that is not necessary," I said, trying to hide my joy at having been freed at last while sparing everyone's sensibilities.

"Indeed," Frollo echoed. "As Esmeralda's host, it is my duty to see to her comfort, which I'm ashamed to admit I've neglected in this instance."

"As ruler of the First Circle, I am her host as well," Seraph said, his gaze slightly hardened.

I fought the urge to roll my eyes, having no patience for their little pissing contest. However, this time, I wished Frollo would escort me back so that he could seize the opportunity to look in on Kwazeem.

"Furthermore," Phoebus continued in a taunting voice before Frollo could respond, "your dignitaries are getting antsy. Some of their cities are hungry for those replenished Relays."

Frollo cast a swift glance at the dignitaries sitting further down on each side of the table. They were indeed stealing furtive glances at him, looking mightily eager to make eye contact with him.

"I guess I might as well head out then," Frollo replied with a slightly clipped tone before rising to his feet. He looked briefly towards the temple, anger fleeting over his handsome features as he no doubt thought of Kwazeem. Turning back to me, he stared at me with an unreadable expression. "You have blessed our city this night. On behalf of our citizens and of the peripheral cities, please accept my sincere gratitude. I had wished to present you to our constituents for these Orbs Ceremonies, but I hope it might happen next time. Rest well, Esmeralda, and I will see you on the morning after next."

With the same disturbing familiarity he had demonstrated before, Frollo took my hand, lifted before him, and kissed my knuckles. I responded with a strained smile but didn't miss how Phoebus stiffened at this inappropriate behavior which implied a greater degree of intimacy between us than truly existed. Not wanting to make a scene with so many people around us, I pinched my lips and kept quiet again as he turned around to leave.

"Wait!" I shouted after Frollo, suddenly remembering something. "Will you not see to Kwazeem first?"

I winced and mentally kicked myself at the same time his name left my lips. Frollo barely managed to hide his shock. Despite him schooling his features, I'd grown to know him enough since my arrival to recognize the seething anger boiling inside of him. While I didn't fear for myself—he didn't own or control me—I worried he might punish Kwazeem for having disobeyed his orders not to speak with me. Frollo had never mentioned Kwazeem's name in my presence. There was only one way I could know it.

"My gardener has broken every single one of our agreements," Frollo said between his teeth. "I will deal with him upon my return. In the meantime, he can reap what he sowed."

"But—"

"I will not discuss this further. Please, do not meddle in my affairs," he interrupted me before I could plead on Kwazeem's behalf.

Without another word, the Praetor turned on his heel and marched towards the dignitaries. They closed in around him like a famished flock of vultures, impatient to bring the Light of Vesta to their respective constituents.

Anger and resentment burned within me that Frollo should so callously deny Kwazeem the assistance he needed. How could he not understand the need for freedom, the thirst to be part of something greater rather than be trapped in eternal isolation? How could he punish him for just wanting to live a little?

Phoebus's intense gaze on me forced me to rein in my emotions. The High Seraph was far too perceptive. To my relief, he didn't question me about that last exchange. I would have hated to be forced to lie to him.

"Shall I take you to your quarters then?" Phoebus asked, his expression unreadable.

"Yes, please."

To my shock, instead of walking by my side the short distance to the temple, Phoebus wrapped his strong arms around me and pressed me against him. With a powerful flap of his wings, he took flight. My hands instinctively clasped behind his neck. His glowing eyes bore into mine as we slowly rose above the plaza. I could barely breathe, not out of fear he would drop me, but intimidated by his intensity. Once more, Phoebus's breathtaking beauty struck me, with silky golden hair falling to his shoulders, pale blue eyes, a straight, noble nose, and a square jaw. And yet, even with the tingling in my skin provoked by his divine aura, he didn't stir me the way Kwazeem did.

"You have awakened within me emotions no other female ever has," Phoebus said with his deep, purring voice that washed over me like a lover's caress. "In all my years as High Seraph, I've never met a Vestal—or any other woman for that matter—who has remained so indifferent to my presence. It is humbling and, in this specific instance, also heartbreaking because you call to me as only a mate would."

My heart constricted at the candor of his words. "You honor me beyond words, High Seraph."

He snorted sadly. "And yet, you do not wish to become my consort."

He'd spoken those words matter-of-factly, without condemnation or bitterness, merely a sad acceptance. I opened and closed my mouth a few times, looking in vain for an appropriate, but gentle response.

"Tell me," Phoebus continued, "and please be honest. Do I displease you? Do I leave you indifferent? Or is there another?"

I licked my lips nervously as we hovered near the balcony to my room. "Every young woman on Obscura dreams of meeting the High Seraph Phoebus. Like them, I, too, hoped for the tremendous honor to find enough grace in your eyes that you would wish for me as your life companion. You are, in the flesh, beyond even the wildest of my imaginings. You have surpassed all of my expectations."

Phoebus's arms ever so slightly tightened around me, pressing me further against his muscular body. His face drew closer to mine and, for a moment, I feared he would kiss me. But he merely continued to examine my features as if they held the key to a great secret.

"And yet, you will not have me," he said at last, looking pensive. "What manner of man managed to snag your heart before I could?"

"A good man who got dealt a terrible hand."

He nodded slowly then effortlessly landed onto my balcony. The High Seraph held me in his arms for a few more seconds before releasing me with obvious reluctance.

"Thank you for the ride," I said, feeling awkward.

He didn't respond, content to stare at me a while longer. After a beat, Phoebus lifted his left arm in front of him and removed what I'd thought to merely be a gem adornment on the golden armband he wore.

"This may serve as a com system or GPS tracker," Phoebus said, holding the device in front of my face. "Should you ever need me, if you are lost, or in the unlikely event you realize what a perfect partner I would be for you, press and hold here for a couple of seconds, and I will hurry to your side."

My throat tightened at such kindness. I once more looked up at him, so tall and massive, with his divine face and majestic wings framing him. To think this delightful male—this god— could be mine and could make me nearly immortal. But my heart lay elsewhere.

"Thank you, High Seraph. You are the kindest of males."

He snorted derisively. "No, beautiful Esmeralda. What I am is jealous of a man I don't even know. Another first for me. You are crushing my ego. And please, call me Phoebus."

I chuckled and gave him a sheepish look. But my smile

quickly faded at the hungry, predatory look he gave me. With lightning speed, Phoebus cupped my face and pressed his lips to mine. Although the gesture startled me, it didn't scare me. Despite the underlying desire I could feel raging beneath, the kiss was almost chaste and definitely controlled. It ended seconds after it started. Phoebus straightened and caressed my lips with two knuckles, a sad look on his face.

Then spreading his four wings, he took flight without another word. His imposing silhouette circled around the plaza. The other Elohim jumped from the perches they had returned to after the feast and circled the plaza one more time with him. They then rose high into the night sky towards the glowing city of Elysium. As they turned into tiny dots in the distance, the Grand Magistrate's barge, a large, boomerang-shaped vessel, took flight carrying Frollo and the dignitaries.

Discarding my flashy ceremonial outfit, I jumped into the shower to wash away the sweat of the Festival's dance. I also hoped that the time it took me to cleanse myself and change would have convinced whatever guard might be spying on me that I had indeed gone to bed like a good girl.

Once dressed in a dark sarong wrapped as a halter dress, I rushed to the lift, flew it down to the ground floor, and then snuck into the backyard through one of the back exits. The beam of the Well's tower lit the area far too much for my liking. Thankfully, the population was too busy dancing and singing to pay attention to me lurking in the shadows. I ran through the garden to the secret passage leading to Kwazeem's house. Finding the cabin plunged in darkness had my anxiety cranking up a notch. I raced to his front door and knocked before turning the knob. Although relieved to find it unlocked, it also greatly disturbed me.

"Kwazeem?" I called out while closing the door behind me. The desolate chirping of an imp startled me. "Victus?" I half-shouted, rushing down the hallway in the direction it had emanated from.

The bedroom stood wide open, giving me a glimpse of a male form sprawled on his stomach on top of his bed. Despite the darkness, enough light trickled in through the window for me to recognize Kwazeem still wearing his costume. Anger surged through me that the guard had so rudely—if not cruelly—tossed him on the bed without taking a moment to check his condition, or if he was in distress.

I instinctively ran my hand over a glowstone at the entrance of the room, which immediately lit up the whole space. Victus and Lazarus, perched on each of Kwazeem's shoulders, appeared to have sunk their claws into him, a distraught expression on their small faces. Their glowing eyes and the energy swirling in the room indicated they were using their limited magic on him, probably to heal or appease.

"Oh, Kwazeem," I whispered, my heart aching for him.

Victus chirped at me, his big eyes staring at me pleadingly as I kneeled on the bed by my man. The muffled sound of tortured moans reached me through his mask. At first, the difficulty in removing it baffled me. It was as though the mask had been taped to his face. But when I finally managed to rid him of it, shock and fear washed over me.

Kwazeem's face was beyond swollen and covered in purplish blotches. Had he not previously explained to me the symptoms of his condition, I would have believed without hesitation that the guards who had escorted him here had beaten him to a pulp for disobeying.

"You can't stay like this for two days," I whispered to myself, before raising my voice. "Kwazeem, can you hear me? It's me, Mera. I'm right here. I want to help you. What can I do to help you?"

His eyelids fluttered, but his puffy eyelids prevented him

from opening them. "F… Fr…" he stuttered, unable to form the word.

"Frollo?" I asked. "He's gone on the Orbs tour, my darling. He won't be back for two days."

Tears gathered in my eyes seeing his battered face take on an even more tortured expression, his hands fisting the bedding as he realized how long he would be subjected to this agony. Kwazeem didn't need me to tell him Frollo was deliberately punishing him.

"Maybe I can do what he does for you?" I offered. "Just tell me what to do, and I will."

But even as I spoke those words, I could see that he wouldn't be able to give me coherent instructions in his current state. Victus chirped, drawing my attention to him then pointing at Kwazeem's hump.

"Do you know what to do?" I asked the imp against hope.

He gave me a sharp nod of the head, then performed all kinds of gestures in his sign language that I didn't understand. Scrunching his face in frustration, he pointed at the hump again. Although I didn't quite know what to do, I remembered Kwazeem mentioning a liquid accumulating in his back. I needed to drain it out.

Even drowning in debilitating pain, my man tried to resist when I removed the costume's cloak and deactivated the holographic suit he had on. Instead of the flowy shirts he usually wore in my presence, a skin-tight, black t-shirt molded his muscular body and the sizeable hump on his back. When I lifted the hem to expose his back, Kwazeem became extremely agitated, groaning in protest through his moans of pain.

"Stop it, you silly man!" I said in a stern voice. "You have nothing to be embarrassed or ashamed of. You are *my* man, and in my eyes, you are the most beautiful male I have ever laid eyes upon, hump included. The High Seraph himself asked me to be his consort tonight, but all I could see was you. So, cut it out. I will not let you pointlessly suffer."

A strange expression I couldn't define settled on his face still scrunched in pain. A single tear slipped down his cheek while his hand blindly reached for me. I took it, and he squeezed mine hard enough to hurt. The shadow of a trembling smile stretched his lips for a second before he winced in pain.

*My poor love.*

Leaning forward, I kissed the tear on his cheek, then brushed my lips against his.

"Let me take care of you, my love," I whispered, caressing his hair. "Whatever the future holds, we'll face it together, you and me. But you have to let me in."

Kwazeem stopped fretting, the same powerful emotion crossing his features as he squeezed my hand again, this time in concession. Removing my hand from his grasp with much reluctance, I went back to lifting his shirt above his hump. My jaw dropped, and my breath caught in my throat at the sight it revealed.

Unlike the humps I'd seen in my research, Kwazeem's wasn't smooth skin on each side of his deformed spine. It was lumpy and glowed as if a constellation had been trapped beneath the skin. I couldn't even see the vertebrae of his spine past the small of his back where his hump began. But right there, at its very base, a large lump glowed like a midnight sun. Whatever Kwazeem's condition was, this was no normal hump.

Unable to resist, my palm reached for it. I gasped as a bolt of Divine Light exploded inside of me. Pleasure almost too unbearable to withstand coursed through me. My nipples hardened painfully, and moisture pooled between my thighs as my inner walls throbbed and contracted with need. My power surged deep within, rattling like a caged beast to pour out of me.

Kwazeem's cry of agony snapped me out of the near

orgasmic state I was teetering in. Clawing at his bedding, he clumsily attempted to crawl away from me… from my touch.

*I'm hurting him!*

I yanked my hand away from him and stumbled a few steps back, horrified.

"St… stop!" Kwazeem cried out. "P… Pow…"

"My power!" I exclaimed, understanding finally dawning on me. "My power is hurting you!"

Even as Kwazeem struggled to acquiesce, the imps frantically nodded their heads. I clamped down on my power, silencing my Divine Light. My man immediately relaxed, and he collapsed on the bed, shaking with pain, his feverish body drenched in sweat.

"I'm sorry, my love. I'm so sorry. I didn't realize," I rambled, feeling horrible for having increased his suffering. "I see the lump you've been talking about. Where is the needle to drain it out?"

Victus chirped and gestured wildly for me to follow him.

"You know where to find it?" I asked. Victus nodded vigorously and gestured again for me to follow. I turned to Kwazeem and caressed his hair. "Victus is going to show me where to get the needle, okay?" I whispered in his ear. "I will come back soon. Hang in there for me, my love. All right?"

Kwazeem feebly nodded his head. Chest constricted, I kissed his lips and then his temple before hastening after Victus, while Lazarus resumed pushing his magic into my man. It didn't take me long to realize the imp was taking me to Frollo's lab. But as we approached its door on the third floor of the temple's spire, I began to wonder how we would break into it. When we reached it, Victus gestured for me to stay put then flew away, down the balcony. As the seconds and then minutes ticked by, I grew increasingly worried that one of the Maidens or the guards would enter the temple and find me lurking outside Frollo's lab.

I nearly jumped out of my skin when the red light on the

door's digital lock turned green with a high-pitched beep, then slid open. Victus grinned his sharp teeth at me before waving me in. I realized then he had entered through one of the windows. Lucky for us, no experiment had been ongoing that might have required Frollo to put the room on lockdown, or seal it to prevent contamination, be it incoming or outgoing.

Despite my curiosity, I didn't waste time in examining the various paraphernalia he had laid about, although the place was very clean and orderly. Victus danced around a closed case. I opened it and found a scary looking syringe with five large vials that seemed to attach to the base of the syringe. Temperature-control lids also sat next to each of the vials. Closing the case, I picked it up and turned towards the imp.

"Anything else?" I asked.

He pointed at a cooling unit by one of the counters and indicated a small jar that I immediately recognized as a potent painkiller often used as anesthetic. I picked it up as well as sterile applicators, an antiseptic solution, and some gauze.

Victus flying to the door confirmed we had everything. With him in the lead, we rushed back to Kwazeem's cabin, relieved that the festivities were still in full swing. Despite the swelling deforming his features, the hopeful look on my man's face when we reentered his room almost made me choke up again.

"Hang in there, sweetie. I'm going to try to do this right," I said.

My hands shook a little as I began to clean his lower back with the antiseptic where the scars of former puncture wounds could be seen. When I applied the anesthetic, Kwazeem's moan of relief filled my heart with both joy at helping my man and anger at Frollo for abandoning him to such torment just to make a point. The anesthetic didn't fully relieve him of all pain, but it appeared to have numbed the main cause of his suffering.

Assembling what resembled a giant spinal tap needle proved easy enough. Under the guidance of Victus, I didn't attach a tube to the back of the syringe right away but waited until I had inserted the needle in Kwazeem's back. Nothing ever terrified me more. What if I hit a nerve and permanently crippled him?

However, the lump where Victus indicated for me to insert it only contained the fluid that had been torturing Kwazeem. As soon as I plugged the tube at the back of the needle, a silvery liquid pulsating with a constellation of stars poured into it. In the second it took me to barely manage to clamp down on my power trying to explode out of my chest again, Kwazeem's body had stiffened from the pain I was causing him.

In a blink, the first vial was filled. I detached it from the syringe, sealed it with the temperature-controlled cork, and then placed it back inside the case. As I began to fill the second vial, my head spun from staring at what I knew beyond any doubt to be Divine Light pouring out of my mate in liquid form. It called to me with a violence that made me dizzy. By the third vial, I was holding it with the costume's cloak wrapped around my hand to dampen the intoxicating contact.

With each vial I filled, tension drained from Kwazeem's body and the lights glowing beneath his lumpy hump faded. However, even after using all five of the vials, I could see a bit more of the fluid remained. A sixth vial would have been required to fully rid him of what should have instead made him akin to a god.

But even as I removed the needle, cleaned the wound, and bandaged it with some gauze, the pieces of the puzzle all started to fall into place. The anger I previously felt towards Frollo's cruel punishment now turned into blind fury. But the time for reckoning would come soon enough. I closed the case and placed it on the dresser on the opposite side of the room.

Settling back down on the bed, closer to Kwazeem's head, I brushed his damp hair away from his face. My lips parted in shock at the sight of the swelling having already reduced by half and the purple bruising fading at record speed before my very eyes.

"Thank you," Kwazeem said in a weak voice. The gratitude and the love in his silver eyes made me melt from the inside out.

"Don't mention it," I said, suddenly feeling shy. "I wouldn't have been much help without Victus," I added, casting an affectionate glance towards the little imp. He chirped proudly, puffed his small, scaly chest, and spread out his wings. "But Lazarus helped, too, keeping watch and pouring his magic into you."

The second imp, who'd been looking a little forlorn for being left out, perked up at being acknowledged as well.

"Are you hungry? Thirsty?" I asked.

"Water, please."

"Right away," I said, scurrying to the kitchen.

It took me a moment to find the glasses, and I ended up pouring myself one as well. I returned to the room to find Kwazeem sitting up, looking groggy as he tried to strip out of his remaining clothes.

"Let me help you," I exclaimed, fighting the urge to scold him for making so much effort, so soon.

"Don't worry," Kwazeem said, although he didn't reject my assistance. "I'm used to managing on my own after a drain. But thank you. I appreciate your help."

He removed everything but his form-fitting black underwear. I tried not to stare at the impressive bulge at his crotch. If it was this big when he wasn't aroused, how massive would it be once erect? But now wasn't the time to entertain naughty thoughts.

Kwazeem sat at the edge of the bed, looking on the verge of complete exhaustion. I handed him the glass of water which he gulped down in the time it took me to take only a couple of sips from mine. Without hesitation, I extended my glass towards him. He hesitated before accepting it with a sheepish smile. I chuckled when he guzzled it down just as quickly as the previous one.

"Do you want more?" I asked, ready to go refill both glasses.

"No, Mera," Kwazeem said in a soft voice. "I only want to rest for a while, and to hold you close while I do, if you would allow it."

Without hesitation, I kicked off my sandals, waved my hand in front of the glowstone to turn it off, and then joined my man in bed. Kwazeem made me lie down on my back and, placing a possessive arm over my midsection, kissed my lips before resting his head on my shoulder. The imps settled at the foot of the bed while I gently caressed my man's hair. Only after his breathing became regular did I also succumb to the lure of the dream world.

# CHAPTER 11
## KWAZEEM

I awoke to soft warmth and the delectable scent of my woman. It took me a moment to realize I wasn't still dreaming, and then the peaceful beating of Esmeralda's heart slightly picked up. Her hand, caressing my back, hesitated for half a beat before resuming its slow tidal movement.

*Not my back, my hump.*

I stiffened at the realization, my insecurities coming back with a vengeance. Having no doubt sensed my reaction, my woman slipped her left hand into my hair, gently scraping my scalp with her nails before pressing her lips at the top of my head.

*She has seen my hump last night, drained it of the poison killing me, and still decided to lie with me.*

In how many more ways did I expect her to keep proving she didn't care about my deformity? Taking a deep breath, I lifted my head resting on her shoulder to lock gazes with her. Whatever I might have feared immediately vanished as I drowned in the green sea of her eyes, and the infinite tenderness burning within.

"My mate," I whispered.

She smiled and cast a swift glance at my lips. I didn't resist the implied invitation. I pressed my lips against hers, and Esmeralda's embrace immediately tightened around me. Timid at first, our kiss deepened, and then our tongues mingled. A hot flame lit up in the pit of my belly as I climbed on top of my woman. She didn't balk, spreading her legs instead for me to settle between them.

Breaking the kiss, my mouth roamed along her jawline, down her neck, stopping only long enough to suck on her pulse there. The link between us awakened, attempting to form again. But no sooner had it reared its head than I felt Esmeralda shut it down on her end. I hated that we couldn't form a proper bond. And yet, if that was the only way we could be together, I would accept it.

Esmeralda's hands feverishly explored my body, and her throaty sighs as my own caressed hers with increasing boldness quickly distracted me from such somber thoughts. When my palm slipped under the short skirt of her sarong dress, I interrupted the kisses I'd been sprinkling over her chest to look up at her. My mate's green eyes, darkened with desire, locked with mine.

No words were needed between us for her to understand my unspoken question.

She responded as silently by reaching for the knot at the back of her neck which kept the sarong wrapped around her body. My mouth went dry when, once she'd untied it, Esmeralda merely tugged on the silky, black fabric, and it obediently parted. A bolt of lust exploded in my nether region at the sight of her flawless, golden skin and her bare, perky breasts whose darker nipples stood erect, begging for my attention.

I didn't resist. My tongue licked her areola in slow circles before I sucked in the hard little bud. My woman's back arched, pressing her breast against my hungry mouth, and her fingers fisted my hair to keep me in place. Flicking away the panel of her sarong that still clung to Esmeralda's body, I wrapped a possessive arm around her back, holding her to me. My free hand caressed her other breast, tweaking its nipple, and then slid down her waist and over the rounded curve of her bum.

Since Esmeralda landed on Eden, every night and every waking hour I'd fantasized of holding her like this, my mouth and hands ravishing her, and hers all over me. Never would I have imagined the incommensurable softness of her skin or her delectable sweet and salty taste on my tongue. In fact, never would I have believed one such as me could earn the favors of any woman, least of all this embodiment of feminine perfection.

Heart pounding with need and a sense of trepidation, I hooked my fingers around the waist of her slip and slowly slid it down, giving her a chance to resist. But she lifted her behind instead to ease my task. My cock further stiffened in response and began to throb with anticipation.

Seeming as impatient as I, Esmeralda kicked off her thong once I had it down to her ankles. With a determination I hadn't expected, my mate's hands reached for my shorts and yanked them down. Because of my height and her shorter arm reach, she didn't get them down too far. Frustrated to break physical contact with my woman for even a second, I kneeled to rid myself of the annoying garment. But Esmeralda didn't wait for me to finish, sitting up to draw my face to hers and resume kissing me.

Falling back down, she pulled me with her while I scrambled to kick off my own underwear.

"Make me yours," she whispered, her cheeks flushed and her lips swollen by my kisses.

My blood rushed to my groin, and the surge of lust that exploded in the pit of my stomach almost had me ram myself inside my mate in one powerful thrust. Reining myself in never felt as miserable as in this instant. I crushed her lips with a passionate kiss, slipping a hand between us to touch her sex.

Wet, warm, and inviting, I inserted a couple of fingers within, dipping in and out of her while my thumb rubbed her clitoris.

"Yes," she moaned, the raspy sound of her voice making me insane with desire.

I should be preparing her more to receive me, but I didn't trust myself to remain in control much longer. However, my girth wouldn't penetrate such a tight sheath with ease.

"Forgive me," I whispered, as I placed the tip of my shaft against her opening.

Esmeralda tensed slightly, her breath catching in her throat as I began to push myself in with shallow thrusts. Eyes locked with my mate, a connection almost magical formed between us. It wasn't the power link that had caused me so much pain and pleasure, but something spiritual. The way she looked at me, with so much tenderness, almost adoration, turned me upside down.

Despite my impatience to be fully one with her, my protective instincts towards my mate made it far easier to control my urges than expected. With infinite care, I breached her hymen and continued my shallow movements until she'd taken all of me.

"You are so beautiful, my mate," I said, covering her face with soft kisses while giving her time to adjust to me. "You are everything to me, Mera. Everything."

"I am yours, Kwazeem," she said, gripping my hair with both hands. "I knew you were the one from the first time I saw you. Even a god couldn't take me away from you. There can never be another but you for me."

"My love," I said, overwhelmed with emotion.

Crushing her lips with a kiss in which I poured all the love she inspired in me, I began to pump in and out of her. Our moans mingled as the most exquisite pleasure turned my blood to liquid fire with each stroke. My claws dug into the mattress as I struggled to control my pace through the endless waves of bliss crashing over me. Esmeralda was so warm, so tight, squeezing my cock from all sides. Her hands clawing at my scales, her blissful sighs spurring me on, I wanted to pound into her like the wild beast that had awakened inside me.

When she began to meet me thrust for thrust, I gradually accelerated the pace, until both of us gave in to our passion with reckless abandon. The slapping sound of our flesh colliding filled the room, accompanied by the creaking of my bed, our blissful moans, and barely intelligible words of love. The burning feel of Esmeralda's skin against my own rivaled the inferno raging inside of me. As my woman began to crest, her slender body shook beneath me. She suddenly seized, her back arching violently over the bed. Her nails digging viciously into my back, my mate cried out my name as she climaxed.

I shouted as her inner walls clamped down on my cock, trying to wrest my own orgasm out of me. Despite my excruciating need to fill my mate with my seed, I couldn't stop riding her. As her sex continued to contract and spasm around my shaft, I abandoned any semblance of control I still possessed and unleashed my passion with something akin to fury. I pounded into her with near savagery, wanting to wreck her, to brand her, to possess all of her down to her very soul. Esmeralda writhed beneath me, chanting my name in an endless litany interspersed with strangled cries that drove me even more insane.

Beneath it all, her power reawakened, hungrily seeking the one dormant within me. Her Divine Light poured inside of me like liquid ecstasy as our link reformed, shattering the last of my restraint. Throwing my head back, I roared my release, and my essence erupted out of me in a searing flow of pleasure, filling my mate. Pain surged at the base of my spine, but I ignored it as I continued to rock in and out of my woman, spilling every drop of my seed.

I gorged on her Divine Light with an insatiable hunger, fueling the power that had lurked within the darkest depths of me. It burned like a living sun, turning my blood to a sea of lava and setting my body ablaze. But even as the pain grew, my power—my lover's power now mine—seemed to burn it right away, pushing me to leech even more from her.

Infused with god-like power coursing through my veins, time and space lost all meaning. My cock hardened again as I continued to plow into the trembling, delicate body beneath me —into the source of infinite ecstasy that had robbed me of coherent thoughts.

I would ravage and consume her, destroy and devour her... All that she is, the Light that burned so bright within her would be mine.

The distant chirping of one of my imps drew me out of my slumber. I felt refreshed, rejuvenated, my body tingling with an excess of energy. I opened my eyes to the mesmerizing sight of my mate's naked form curled against me. She looked good enough to eat with her golden skin contrasting so beautifully against my bluish-grey complexion. I ran a possessive hand down her back, and then rested my palm against the provocative curve of her bum. Blood rushed to my groin as my insatiable hunger for her reawakened.

For a moment, I considered waking her to once more claim what was mine and mine alone. The memory of her moans in my ears, of her burning body writhing beneath my sensual assault, and of the tight grip of her sex stroking my cock as I pounded into her was driving me insane.

*Enough!*

It took all my willpower to settle for a chaste kiss on her temple before pulling away from her. My shaft stood painfully erect as I gazed at the perfection sleeping trustingly in my bed. I had been relentlessly greedy in my lust last night and feared it would be a long time before my endless appetite abated where she was concerned. I would have to be careful not to drive her away with my excessive needs.

Despite the peaceful way she slept, I could feel Esmeralda's weariness. How could she not be exhausted? Beyond me keeping her awake through most of the night in a frenzied sex marathon, my woman had singlehandedly filled the Well of Power in a Festival of Light that would go down as the most remarkable in history. She needed rest. Thankfully, Frollo was absent until the morrow, and everyone else was probably passed out in a drunken stupor from last night's revelries. Therefore, my mate could sleep in my bed to her heart's content with no one looking for her.

A dip in the river would have been nice but, as I tended to linger in the water swimming against the stream to loosen any stiffening in my back, I chose to take a shower instead. After checking that my woman still slept, I quickly dressed and went to pick a single sarnokia, a dusty blue, long-petaled flower, with iridescent pistils that made the cup of the flower look as if a galaxy swirled within. Extremely hard to grow, they were the ultimate gift from a lover to his soulmate. After placing it in a vase on the nightstand, I kissed my goddess' lips before heading out with my bow.

Victus and Lazarus rushed to my side the minute I stepped out of the house, chirping happily and multiplying the congratulations and kind words at having bonded with my mate. I thanked them in turn for their discretion exiting the room when things had started to heat between us last night. It suddenly struck me that soon, both my little friends would leave my side to seek their own mates. Although imps rarely formed couples other than to reproduce and didn't raise their own offspring—who happened to be self-sufficient from birth—there were no guarantees my companions wouldn't choose to remain with their species.

The fear of losing Esmeralda compounded that uncertainty.

Even as I moved through the surrounding forest at a slow jog, thoughts of the impossibility of my relationship with my mate tormented me. She couldn't claim me before the citizens of Paris without condemning me to a certain death, and maybe even Frollo. If she told him about us, he would completely lose it and forbid us from seeing each other.

*He doesn't own me or her. We do not have to obey.*

He couldn't rat us out without exposing his role in my presence here. But Esmeralda couldn't live in my cabin with me without eventually raising suspicions with her frequent comings and goings.

*Would he let me return to the temple and share her quarters, or let her share mine?*

I couldn't imagine him allowing it, not with his ego. To have been bested by me, a Fallen, in the affections of the most powerful Vestal to have set foot on the First Circle in our lifetime would wound his pride too deeply. But even without that, sharing her quarters would be too risky with visiting dignitaries using some of the rooms on that same floor, not to mention the cleaning staff.

*If only I hadn't been a half-breed...*

Victus and Lazarus crisscrossing in front of me at high speed forced me to slow down. I'd been so lost in thought that I'd been stomping around the woods loudly enough to scare any game or prey to be had. I inwardly cursed myself and focused my natural long-range vision on my surroundings, looking for a target. It took a while before I spotted the dark fur of a chisawni; an herbivorous creature the size of a medium dog, but that looked like the offspring a beaver and a rabbit would produce.

It would provide enough meat for the imps and me for the next week, even if Esmeralda also shared our meals. Its leather would go to making the scabbards of my next weapons, and its teeth and bones would serve to make tools and more weapons. Whatever remained, the imps would devour.

Taking aim with my arrow, hoping for a clean kill, the energy that had tingled inside me since I woke up suddenly sparked to life. I stared in wonder as the same electric tendrils that had appeared around our hands the first time Esmeralda and I touched manifested around my wrist, over my hand before infusing the arrow I had just nocked. A wistful smile stretched my lips realizing my woman had become a part of me since our mating. No wonder I'd felt like a god all morning.

Itching to return to her as soon as possible, I refocused on my prey only to be startled by the appearance of a smaller pair of bunny ears, hopping around the larger chisawni. The little kit rubbed its tiny face against what had to be its parent who flapped its flat, beaver tail in approval. Cursing again, I lowered my arrow and glared at Victus who chirped mockingly at my annoyance.

"I guess we're having fish," I muttered, shouldering my bow.

The electric coils around my hand faded, and the energy thrumming inside me went back into what felt like sleeping mode. Although I wasn't quite equipped for fishing, I headed straight to the river, planning on using one of my arrows as a spear. The imps flew ahead to survey the shallow banks where various respectable-sized fish liked to swim. By the time I caught up with them, Victus and Lazarus were already frantically circling an area ripe for the picking. I stepped on the rocks surrounding the shallow nook where half a dozen silver mullet fish were frolicking.

Fishing was always a little too easy here. But I had wanted to impress my woman with my hunting skills and my ability to provide, whatever the situation. It was silly in this day and age where everything was abundant except energy. Still, I had too little to offer compared to her. Any points I could score mattered.

Fisting one of my arrows like a spear, I targeted the largest fish and struck. As soon as my arrow found its mark, a bolt of lightning blasted out of my hand, zapping the five other nearby fish that had attempted to flee. I yelped and recoiled, almost losing my footing on the slippery rocks. I gaped at my hand and then at the five fish floating belly up around the one I had 'speared.' The imps hooted with joy and licked their thin lips in anticipation. Recovering from my shock, I grabbed my unexpected haul by the tails, three in each hand, then made my way back home.

I dropped the fish in the sink before going to check on Esmeralda. She was still fast asleep. Despite my urge to go kiss her, I exited the room quietly, not wanting to stink her up with my fishy smell. I cut one of the mullets in two and gave each of my imps a half. They chomped away at their meal, devouring everything: scales, bones, and offal. Shaking my head in amusement, I cleaned, filleted, and deboned the remaining mullets. I rubbed them with some spices and herbs then set them in the cooling unit while waiting for my mate to wake up.

After washing off the fishy stench that had clung to me, I headed to my forge. Although my hammering would be loud, I'd soundproofed my bedroom because of the many events that regularly took place on the plaza. With the music and clamor from last night's Festival, it would have been impossible for us to sleep otherwise as the noise carried all the way here.

While gardening allowed me to surround myself with the grace and beauty that I lacked, blacksmithing was my true passion. Wielding the hammer, shaping metal, and bending it to my will always gave me a tremendous sense of power and control that otherwise escaped me in this life. Knowing that the weapons I made surpassed those of the best craftsman in the city filled me with tremendous pride.

Vestals often wielded a staff of power. But they either bought it in the city they joined, or it was given to them as a gift by the Praetor or Elohim who took them as consort. I intended to build one myself for my Esmeralda. In my mind's eye, I could already see the intricate details it would have. That staff would be my masterpiece.

The challenge would be getting my hands on the gems I wished to ornate it with. Frollo usually never balked at providing me with whatever material or resources I asked for. Being a male of simple needs, my requests had always been reasonable. So much in fact that he'd often brought me far better quality than I asked, for example with my mattress and pillows. Those little acts of unexpected kindness made it difficult for me to hate Frollo.

In truth, I didn't quite know how I felt about him. It was a strange mix of love and hate.

Glowstones and lumis he would bring me without question, in whatever quantities, shapes, and sizes I required. But I wanted jade or emeralds to match the color of my woman's eyes. I would need to think on ways to achieve that goal without getting caught.

Staring at the various metals at my disposal, I reached for a large piece of tarantium—a light but extremely sturdy metal used to make the finest weapons. As a Vestal, Esmeralda would have undergone battle training in case she became consort to an Elohim. While the interplanetary wars had mostly waned over the past decade, trouble constantly brewed in our solar system. It was only a matter of time before another conflict forced the winged warriors to intervene. As Elohim and Vestals mutually enhanced their powers, together they became an unstoppable force.

Even though Esmeralda would never go to the front, and despite the fact that Vestals mostly battled with lightning, I would insert a long, viciously sharp blade at each end of her staff. Hers would surpass any weapon ever wielded by one of the daughters of Vesta.

With my forge burning hot, I heated the metal until it became pliable. I then picked up my hammer and turned to my anvil to start shaping. At the first strike of the hammer against the piece of tarantium, my power awakened with fury, electric coils wrapping all around my upper chest and the length of my arms. Like a living thing, the energy slithered and writhed over the metal, infusing it with its essence. A bright vein streaked the dark metal —partially red from the heat.

I paused and stared at my hand in awe and then at the metal. Lifting my hammer again, I struck the metal once more with the same result. Galvanized, I hammered away, the energy within me building with each strike. The electric coils faded from my arms in the few minutes I spent at the forge to reheat the metal, only to return as soon as I resumed shaping it. Lightning swirled around me, crackling and sparkling. I felt bigger, stronger, and nearly invincible; very much like a god.

My head jerked left at the sound of a soft gasp. Barefoot, her curly, reddish-brown hair falling loosely on her back, and her sarong wrapped around her body with a front knot on her chest, Esmeralda stared at me wide-eyed. I stopped hammering and stared right back at her. My heart filled to bursting with an emotion no words could describe. Dropping both my hammer and the tongs with which I'd held the burning metal, I rushed to my woman.

Esmeralda squealed in surprise, then giggled when I lifted her up, spun around a few times before lowering her just enough to kiss her lips. She wrapped her arms around my neck and parted her lips, allowing me to deepen the kiss. When she came up for air, my mate cupped my face and examined my features as if I was the most wonderful treasure she'd ever laid eyes upon. My chest tightened again with love and gratitude that such an amazing woman could see and care for the man trapped in this body.

My mate caressed my cheeks with infinite tenderness. "You're glowing with Divine Light," she whispered, glancing at the electric coils climbing onto her hand still hugging my face.

"*You* are my Divine Light," I replied, my eyes drinking in her beauty.

Esmeralda smiled and rubbed her nose against mine before burying her face in my neck. I tightened my arms around her and for the next few seconds, minutes, or eternity, we held each other in silence. By the time I released her, the electric coils around me had vanished.

"How are you feeling?" I asked, the concern gnawing at me creeping into my voice.

"Wonderfully wrecked?" she said, teasingly.

My cheeks burned with embarrassment while tension drained from my shoulders. "I should have been gentler and less greedy," I said sheepishly.

"Did you hear me complain? Do I look like I am now?" she gently chastised me. "You were better than anything I had ever fantasized for my first time. You were always meant to be the one for me."

My throat tightened again with emotion as I struggled to comprehend how I had earned Esmeralda's affection, she who had been created to be the mate of a god.

"My beautiful mate," I whispered before brushing my lips against hers. "You must be starving. Let me feed you," I said, silencing my reawakening desire.

Wrapping my arm around her shoulders, I tucked her against me, and she wrapped hers around my waist. Once in the dine-in kitchen, I settled her at the table before getting down to business. She offered to help, but I wouldn't have it. After putting the fish steaks on the grill, I prepared some side dishes of stirred vegetables and roasted potatoes.

"How do you get all these ingredients?" Esmeralda asked, while munching on some nuts and berries I'd given her to nibble on until the meal was ready.

"Frollo," I said matter-of-factly.

"Frollo buys your groceries?" Esmeralda exclaimed, her voice disbelieving.

I chuckled at the thought of the Praetor running such menial errands for me. "No," I said, checking on the fish. "I give him a list of my needs, and he passes it off to the cook. Malina runs most of my errands and leaves them in the same location for me, near one of the hidden passages of the temple. That is also where she leaves my meals... or rather did when I still lived in the temple."

"So Malina knows about you?" my woman asked.

I hesitated before shaking my head. "She knows of the gardener who lives in the temple. However, she has no idea I am a Fallen. I doubt she even knows my name. Frollo told her I was a Noletian hybrid."

"Aah, clever!" Esmeralda said. "Half of them develop extreme photosensitivity in their early teenage years while having perfect night sight."

"Correct. And that's why I have a cloak for the few times I need to go into the temple during daylight," I explained. "But, most of the time, I live on a reversed schedule than the rest of the population."

I didn't add that living at night made it easier than staring all day at the life I couldn't partake in. And yet, that hadn't stopped me from watching the population for hours in the early hours of the morning before finally seeking my bed, or in the late afternoon after rising.

"Frollo forbade the staff from seeking me out, stating that a few exposures to sunlight had left me badly scarred, which made me extremely self-conscious."

"He has thought of everything," Esmeralda said pensively.

I didn't need to ask where her thoughts had wandered off to. The same questions that had plagued me earlier were now tormenting her. But in a tacit agreement, we didn't delve into the subject just yet. After I finished preparing our meal, I served us each a plate.

"That smells wonderful, but it's way too much food!" Esmeralda exclaimed at the *very* generous portion I'd given her.

I scratched sheepishly at the scales along my neck. "It's early afternoon. You must be famished. I cannot allow my mate to starve."

She burst out laughing and shook her head at me as if I were silly. "So, instead, you'll stuff me until I get indigestion."

I muttered something mostly unintelligible before apologizing for the lack of fancy tableware, which earned me another 'don't be silly' kind of reaction. Despite her comment about the portion size, my woman dug into her food with a healthy appetite, moaning in delight after the first bite. She ended up devouring more than two-thirds of her plate. I couldn't tell which one of us was the most surprised, but it pleased me she'd enjoyed something I'd made for her this much.

Sadly, our amicable and relaxed chatter as we ate ended too soon.

"I must return to the temple," Esmeralda said with a somber tone.

"Why?" I asked, crestfallen. "Frollo will not return until tomorrow."

"Right, but Malina will have sent food up for me," my mate argued. "While she may not question me sleeping in late, she will grow worried—if not suspicious—if I don't collect the heated food tray outside my room in the next hour or so. She's already too well aware of my gargantuan morning appetite."

"I see," I said, schooling my features not to show how badly her words had crushed me. I'd foolishly imagined we'd spend an entire day together without fear of reprisal.

The commiserating look on her face told me I'd failed miserably at hiding my feelings. Rising to her feet, she circled around the table and settled on my lap.

"Don't look so sad, my love," Esmeralda said, rubbing her nose against mine before kissing my lips. "I'm only going to let them see me a few times in the next hour then ask not to be disturbed for the rest of the day. And then I'll come right back to you."

My heart soared at that news. As much as I hated parting from her even for a minute, one hour would allow me to prepare some romantic escapade for the two of us. I wanted us to enjoy as much of this day as possible before we had to tackle more difficult discussions.

"All right," I said, unable to suppress my beaming smile.

She chuckled again, kissed me with a bit more passion this time, and then reluctantly pulled out of my embrace.

"You are far too tempting, Kwazeem. You will drive me to distraction!"

"And I have no shame about it."

With a heavy heart, I waited for her to retrieve her sandals from the bedroom then escorted her to the entrance of the hidden passage. As I watched her walk down the path alone, an inexplicable sense of doom grew within me with each step taking her farther away from me. When she turned the corner and vanished from view, a single thought replayed in a loop in my head: I would never get her back.

# CHAPTER 12
## ESMERALDA

The minute I walked away from Kwazeem, from his wonderful aura, the weariness that had pestered me all morning returned with a vengeance. My body had never felt so weak before. By the time I reached the elevator, I had to lean against the wall to hold me up. When the lift stopped on my floor, it took every bit of my energy to make it to my door without crawling on all fours. Thankfully, there was no one around to witness my current pathetic state.

I hauled in the hovercart carrying the heated, covered plates the cook had left outside my quarters for me—as expected—and closed the door. With much difficulty, I made a beeline for my bed and collapsed on it. Sprawled on the divine mattress, my feet hanging over the edge, I could have wept with relief. My head swam, and my body tingled with numbness.

Vestals burning out on their first Festival was commonplace. The Matriarchs on Obscura had regularly warned us against pushing too hard to prove ourselves or out of fear of disappointing our host. Considering my phenomenal performance last night—in large part thanks to Kwazeem enhancing me—it wasn't surprising I'd be crashing so hard. But the timing couldn't have been more rotten. Without my mate's aura to sustain me, I would never have the strength to go back to him. He would worry terribly.

*And then he'll come check up on you and see that all is well.*

That slightly appeased me. Kwazeem knew every secret passage in and out of the temple. He would find his way to me without getting noticed. In a way, it might be better if he came here. He could remain out of sight when Malina came knocking again for supper and leave at first light before Frollo returned. Anyway, we would see Frollo's shuttle approach long before it landed, which would give my man plenty of time to return to his cabin.

But, in the long term, that wouldn't be a viable situation.

The questions I had been dodging and avoiding were now demanding to be answered. I'd shamelessly pursued the object of my desires and gotten the man my heart ached for. But where did we go from here?

I didn't want to hide my relationship with the man I loved. Lurking in the shadows, stealing kisses behind closed doors, and sneaking in and out of each other's rooms like adulterers wasn't the future I wanted for us. And, at some point in the future, I would want children with my man.

The citizens of Paris would never accept a Fallen in their midst. If there had been a way to make them accept him, Frollo would have probably seen to it, if only to remove the threat over himself. I hated the thought of leaving Paris. Not only was the city growing on me, but I could make a huge difference for the people living here. As vain as that might sound, I didn't believe any of my other Vestal sisters could handle the needs of this city as I could.

And yet, if it came to a choice between Paris and my man, Kwazeem would win any day.

*We could leave.*

From my recent research, some of the lesser moons were not

as intolerant towards the Fallen. After all, the conflict that had initiated the Fall—the war between the Elohim and their Light Bearers—had started right here, on the First Circle.

As an Anointed, choosing a lesser Circle to work on would raise a lot of suspicions. Worse still, with the tense energy situation here, there would be an uproar amongst the citizens of Paris whom had just regained hope of a brighter future last night. They could retaliate against the planet or moon I settled on with embargoes and tariffs on trade goods. Wealth wasn't an issue in Paris; energy was.

We could also just go live on our own somewhere and leave everything else behind. My family was financially set and secured with the final dowry of my ordainment. Aside from Old Nan—and even then—Kwazeem had nothing holding him here. With my sign-on fee, I had enough credits to buy us a piece of land and everything we might need to build a happy home. Kwazeem was an accomplished hunter and craftsman. I wasn't clumsy with my hands either. Together, we could make it work.

For one foolish instant, I thought of reaching out to Phoebus. I still had the com he'd given me, and he had a good heart beneath that tough exterior. But there was no way he would support me running off with a Fallen, especially considering he wanted me for himself. And going to stay with Althea wasn't an option. Frollo would go to her first to look for us if we just ran away.

*But she could help us secure transportation off world.*

My heart skipped a beat as this thought of Frollo abruptly reminded me that we hadn't returned his draining kit back to his lab. He would be livid once he'd realized we'd not only broken into his lab, but that Kwazeem was also no longer solely dependent on him to treat his condition. Yet another strike against us. I couldn't begin to imagine how he would react to all of this.

*He shouldn't have left Kwazeem to suffer as punishment.*

Be that as it may, it wouldn't benefit us to alienate him more than was necessary.

Too many questions swirled around in my head. My bone deep weariness made it next to impossible for me to focus on a smart solution. Giving in to the call of oblivion, I fell asleep with Kwazeem's face hovering before me.

# CHAPTER 13
## KWAZEEM

For the hundredth time at least, I looked at my clock wondering where Esmeralda was. The sense of unease that had been churning in my gut since she left had only steadily increased with each passing minute. She should only have been gone one hour. More than double that time had elapsed.

I wanted to go check up on her to make sure everything was okay. But doing so at this early hour of the afternoon was beyond risky. The population usually slept in late and most remained home to recover from their hangover the day after the Festival. But that wouldn't keep a respectable number of them—the more moderate ones—from being up and about. What if I ran into one of the Light Maidens, the temple's regular guards, or staff?

*They wouldn't bother me if I were cloaked.*

That settled it. Frollo had made it clear to the staff that they were to leave me alone. As I went to fetch my cloak in my bedroom, I cycled through a series of possible excuses for my presence in the temple if anyone should ask. But even as I turned around to exit my room, my imps came rushing in with a scared squeal and hid under my bed.

My blood instantly turned to ice in my veins. Only Frollo's approach could have stirred such a violent reaction from them.

*But he's not supposed to be back until tomorrow!*

Stuffing my cloak back into the dresser, I hastened into the living area of my cabin. The chiming sound of the bell resonated seconds before the door swished open, revealing a brooding Frollo. Judging by his attire, he'd just returned from one of the peripheral cities and hadn't taken the time to change.

The Praetor's blue gaze slowly roamed over me, his expression betraying a growing seething anger. The absence of surprise at seeing me up and about took me aback. He knew that I should normally be writhing in agony, half passed out from the debilitating pain. And then my stomach dropped with sudden fear. Had he intercepted Esmeralda on her way back here? Was that why she hadn't returned? Had she seen him arrive and wisely decided to stay put?

*But why wasn't he surprised?*

"I shortened my trip to come take care of you, thinking I'd given you sufficient time to contemplate the error of your ways. But here you are, looking as fresh and thriving as those plants you tend," Frollo said in the iciest tone I'd ever heard from him. "Where is she?"

My heart leapt in my chest. He could only be referring to Esmeralda. But why wouldn't he know she was at the temple? Had he not checked her room? Had she not made it back to the temple? That made no sense, it was too short a walk. Had anything happened to her along the way, Frollo would have inevitably run into her while coming here.

"Where's who?" I asked.

"Don't play dumb with me," Frollo hissed, advancing towards me with one menacing step. "You know damn well who I'm talking about."

"There's no one here but me, and now you," I said, lifting my chin defiantly. "If you are referring to the Vestal, she's likely in the temple."

"You are going to pretend she didn't help you with your condition?" Frollo challenged me, his hands fisting spasmodically.

"What makes you think I needed external help?" I argued.

"You couldn't drag your sorry ass to the temple last night because you were too crippled by pain. How the fuck would you have made it back to the temple on your own to break into my lab and steal my syringe case?" Frollo yelled, finally losing any semblance of control.

I flinched, mentally kicking myself for having forgotten to return it to his lab last night. It all made sense now. He'd come home early to relieve me of my pain only to find the case missing from its normal place. I didn't quite know how to feel about that. I hated that he'd used my condition against me to torture me. But was it remorse, a sense of compassion, or some twisted affection towards me that had made him return sooner? As he should have been gone until morning, he naturally assumed Esmeralda would still be with me since she'd defied him to help me.

*And she would have been had she not somehow been detained.*

The need to go check up on her gnawed at me. Considering how tired she'd been, I wanted to believe she'd merely fallen asleep again. I wouldn't be able to rest until I knew for sure.

"Since you'd chosen to let me suffer for days to make a point, she did come to my aid," I snarled back.

"And whose fault was that?" he shouted, before pacing the room. "I was kind by letting you come back to the temple so that you wouldn't miss out on the whole Festival, and this is how you thanked me?"

"You don't own me!" I yelled back. "You are not my father,

and I'm not a slave for you to order about. You do not dictate where I can and cannot go!"

Frollo stared at me disbelieving, as if he was seeing me for the first time. And maybe he was. I had never actually challenged any of his 'orders' before; it had never mattered. But now, his 'protection' chafed. I would not be kept on a leash.

"As long as you are in *my* city, I most certainly do get to dictate where the fuck you're allowed to go." He leveled at me a look with something akin to contempt that had my hackles rising. "As for your father, *that* I'm definitely not, and I have no use for a slave, you ungrateful little shit."

"Could have fooled me," I snapped back.

"Excuse me?" he said, outraged.

"Do you think I cannot guess the worth of the weapons I've made, and which you sell as your own?" I asked in a hard tone. "Would you get as magnificent a garden as the one I've made for you without paying top wages?"

"And what would you do with credits, *Kwazeem*?" Frollo asked in a syrupy voice, saying my name with a certain dose of contempt. "I have provided you with everything you've ever needed, and anything you requested I bought. So, don't you dare play the victim. You'd be dead without me."

"Living by your rules, I might as well be," I retorted.

"My rules are the only reason you're still alive. The plaza was crawling with Elohim," Frollo said between his teeth his voice gradually getting louder. "What the fuck do you think would have happened if they'd gotten to you before my guards did? If you have a death wish, go right ahead and strut your stuff in broad daylight. But you will *not* bring me down with you and least of all her!"

I flinched, aching to shout back at the unfairness of it all, but he was right. My selfish desires could have caused our collective downfall. Fists and teeth clenched, I averted my eyes, breathing heavily to cool my temper.

Frollo exhaled loudly, and some of his anger bled out. "Look, I will not pretend to understand how difficult, isolated, and confining your life must feel. But mingling with others will *never* be a possibility for you. And you *need* to stay away from Esmeralda."

My head jerked up, and I glared at him in outrage. He sustained my gaze, his hard and unwavering.

"I realize that you are no longer a child and that, as an adult male you have certain… needs. It was my failure not to account for that sooner, and I will do my best to remedy that," Frollo said, somewhat stiffly. "But Esmeralda is not for you. She's a stunning woman with a heart of gold. But do not confuse compassion with romantic interest."

I lifted my chin with defiance. "I assure you, Praetor, what Esmeralda feels for me isn't compassion."

He recoiled and stared at me as if I'd lost my mind. "You think she's falling for *you*? You think she would refuse the Grand Magister of Paris *and* the High-Seraph of the Elysium for *you*?"

"I don't *think*, I know," I said with arrogance, a smug smile stretching my lips.

Frollo took a step back, a look of horror slowly dawning on his face. "Kwazeem… what have you done?" he whispered. His face took on a pleading expression that had my stomach knot with worry. "Tell me you haven't touched her? Tell me you did not defile her?"

My anger flared at that last comment. "My love for her, or hers for me isn't vile or foul. You and the rest of the population may not deem me worthy of Esmeralda, but she sees beyond this body. I am not a monster, I am a man!" I shouted, slapping my chest with both palms.

"THIS ISN'T ABOUT SENTIMENTS, YOU FOOL!" Frollo yelled. "You are a Fallen. Your DNA is a death sentence to a Vestal! Do you not remember what started the war between the Elohim and your people?"

I blinked at him, confused. "A Fallen ran away with the previous High Seraph's mate. What does that have to do with anything? Esmeralda wasn't mated to anyone before choosing me."

"Before choosing you…" Frollo breathed out, as if speaking to himself.

Pale, looking almost haggard, he stumbled to the nearest couch and let himself fall into it. I'd never seen him look so crushed, so defeated. The sense of unease came back with a vengeance, laced with a certain amount of hurt. Yes, he had wanted her for himself. But couldn't he even muster a sliver of happiness for me that I could have found my soulmate, against all odds?

Frollo snorted and shook his head with a sad smile. "Tell me Kwazeem, did *your mate* look tired when you last parted ways?"

I stiffened, a sense of dread washing over me as my mind was flooded with images of Esmeralda looking weary as she stood at the entrance of the forge, staring at me.

"She did, didn't she?" Frollo asked, although it was more of a statement. The look of hurt, betrayal, and sadness on his face clawed at me as my anxiety climbed another notch. "You've killed us all, Kwazeem. All three of us."

"Stop with your damn riddles and speak plainly!" I exclaimed at last, exasperated.

"The war didn't start because a Fallen stole High Seraph's Galleus's mate—he would have merely hunted and killed him for that. The war started because Arahzor, the Fallen in question, drained Armina of her Divine Light. Why do you think your people used to be called Light Eaters as often as Light Bearers?" Frollo snapped. "You feed off the Light of the Elohim. Once they'd run away, without the Elohim to feed him, Arahzor devoured all that Armina had, severing her link to Vesta."

"What do you mean?" I whispered, memories of gorging on

Esmeralda's Light as I passionately made love to her flooding my mind. It had been like a drug, a divine nectar that could only pacify the unquenchable thirst within me.

"Meaning that he had turned an Anointed Vestal into a commoner," Frollo spat out. "She was never again able to summon the elements, her ergokinetic powers snuffed out forever." He rose to his feet looking at me with barely contained seething rage. "Do you know what will happen when Esmeralda is unable to perform the Grand Chakra Ceremony on the plaza in two days or any other of her Vestal tasks in the following days? Do you think Phoebus will sit by idly when he finds out the one female he'd wanted as a consort has been thus defiled?"

"But… I have been enhancing her power," I argued feebly, refusing to believe my love for Esmeralda could have caused such a horrible thing.

"There is no such thing as a Fallen—"

"I HAVE!" I repeated forcefully. "Esmeralda has awakened a power inside me I didn't know I had, and she confirmed that *I* have made hers significantly more powerful than ever before. That first night in the chapel while she Chanted, she fed off *my* energy, and hers fueled mine in return, which accelerated my symptoms. At the Festival, that same link formed between us which made her so incredibly powerful, and me so ill, so fast. Even the first time I kissed her, days before the Festival, I hadn't drained her. You must be wrong."

My arguments sounded logical to me, but I was also grasping at straws. If what Frollo had said was true, it would devastate her, and it would crush me.

"For all our sakes, I hope you are right," Frollo said, in a cold voice. "Where's my syringe case?"

Lips pinched, jaw clenched, I bit back the comment that *I* should keep it, not him. But I'd pushed him enough for one day. Anyway, now that I'd finally been able to examine it closely at my leisure, I'd be able to replicate a kit of my own to no longer be at his mercy. With a strategically placed set of mirrors, I might even be able to perform the procedure on my own.

Without a word, I turned on my heel and marched to my bedroom to retrieve the case. After I returned and handed it over to him, I kicked myself mentally for not having disposed of the contents of the vials. Although she hadn't said it in so many words, Esmeralda had hinted at Frollo making use of it in a more than questionable way.

He took the case from my hands, opened it, and examined its contents. The odd glimmer in his eyes as he stared at the vials filled to the brim with the silvery liquid sparkling as if it had captured all the stars in the sky made me further regret I hadn't disposed of it.

"I want you to leave Paris," Frollo said in a calm voice, devoid of emotion.

My heart sank.

"What?" I whispered, staring at him in shock.

"I can no longer trust you not to put all of our lives in danger," Frollo said calmly. "And I especially cannot trust you to stay away from Esmeralda."

"You can't—"

"I'M NOT DONE!" Frollo snapped before continuing in a calm, measured, and calculated tone. "I will contact Althea—Old Nan—to see if she will have you back. If we're lucky, and you haven't ruined Esmeralda, you are never to see her again. I'll come to the Godswood once a month to tend to your back. But if you have done the irreversible, we'll need to get you both off this planet before the mob and the Elohim descend upon you."

"You do not dictate my relationship with Esmeralda or where I go," I said, taking one menacing step towards him. "She is not your prisoner, and neither am I. If I'm no longer welcomed in the temple's ground, I will go where I see fit."

"I don't give a fuck where you go," the Praetor says dismissively. "Go to Godswood, and I will honor my promise to Althea to look after you. Don't, and I wash my hands of your fate. As long as she lives in the temple, Esmeralda is my responsibility and is under my protection. Should she choose to run away with you, I will wash my hands of her as well. But until then, you approach her or the temple, and I will have you arrested for illegal entry in the city."

"Give me away, and they will prosecute you as well," I retorted angrily, hurt by his indifference far more than I'd ever admit.

Frollo snorted and shook his head. "No, silly boy. Do you really think I hadn't planned for the eventuality you might go rogue? No one has ever seen or spoken to my gardener, but me and my two personal guards. On the day you get arrested, the corpse of my disfigured gardener will be found. The poor man will have been brutally murdered by the ruthless Fallen hybrid who infiltrated the city to kidnap and defile its greatest jewel; the people's beloved Anointed Vestal Esmeralda."

I gaped at him, robbed of voice by such a cruel and calculated evil plan.

A hard smile stretched his lips as he coldly stared at me. "You have two days to pack your belongings, at which point my guards will either escort you to the Godswood or kick you out of the city. Your choice." He gave me an assessing once over before continuing. "Whatever you may think, I do not wish you ill. But fuck with me, and I will crush you."

With these last words, he turned around and headed for the door.

"You may kick me from your city, and forbid me access to your temple, but nothing and no one will ever keep me away from my mate," I said in a tone that brooked no argument.

Frollo stopped and looked at me over his shoulder. "Do what

you must, and so will I. Just see that you do not set foot again in the temple."

I do not know how long I stood staring at the door after it closed behind him. A single thought replayed in my mind: please, let Esmeralda be all right.

# CHAPTER 14
## ESMERALDA

I woke up with a start, feeling observed. My head jerked right, and I gasped in shock at the sight of Frollo, sitting in a chair a few meters away from me. His blue eyes looked almost dark as he stared at me with an angry scowl. Pressing my palm to my chest to contain the erratic beating of my heart, I glared at him in outrage that he should trespass the privacy of my room.

And then I noticed the syringe case resting on his lap.

Swallowing hard, my gaze flicked back to his. As my lying down position made me feel too vulnerable, I sat up at the edge of my bed and folded around me the panels of the black sarong I was still wearing. Gone were the seductive looks, smoldering glances, respectful gazes, and open admiration the Praetor had previously showered me with. The blue depths of his eyes burned with a hard mix of anger and contempt. One could almost say hatred.

Was he truly such a sore loser?

"You've been busy," Frollo said at last with an icy voice.

"I merely did what someone else wouldn't," I said, lifting my chin without the slightest remorse.

"Oh, we both know you did far more than that, little Vestal," he retorted with contempt. "But then, are you even a Vestal anymore?"

I recoiled, taken aback by the unexpected comment. "What is that supposed to mean?"

He gave me a slow once over as if examining an odd, alien creature. "Your Light is gone. A rock by the roadside would emit a thousand times more ergokinetic energy than you do," he said bitterly. "You shone with the brightness of the sun. The gods of the Elysium were willing to lay their hearts at your feet. And you threw it all away for the cock of a Fallen."

I gasped in outrage at such rudeness.

"First off, you have no say in my relationship with Kwazeem. And second, you do not get to judge anyone the way you've been whoring around with the Maidens," I snapped in response to his crude words. "My Light isn't gone. I merely overexerted myself at the Festival. It's called a burn out; a very common reaction amongst newly ordained Vestals upon their first Festival."

Even as I spoke those words, a cold shiver ran down my spine. I knew of the burn out but had never experienced it myself —until now. Old Nan's warning had been replaying in my head non-stop since I'd awakened in Kwazeem's bed feeling completely exhausted, and my powers muted.

"I am well aware of the burn out. You seem to forget that I've been Praetor of the greatest city in the Nine Circles for more than a decade," Frollo said, adjusting the case on his lap as he leaned back in the chair. "Many of your sisters have come and gone, each one too weak to fill the Well. All of them burnt out and did so right at the Well during their Chant. You completed the ceremonial, then sat and enjoyed dinner for two hours with us before getting escorted back to your room. You then snuck out to Kwazeem's cabin, drained him, and then fucked him all night. So no, Esmeralda, you did *not* burn out."

"That's enough from you," I shouted, jumping to my feet. Beyond the crass rudeness, his words terrified me far more than I dared admit to myself. "I do not need your approval for anything, and I will not tolerate you trashing my relationship with my man. I do not believe my Light has faded. Last night wasn't my first time being close with Kwazeem. Every time we've been together, he's enhanced my power. Do you really think I did all this on my own at the Festival?"

Frollo narrowed his eyes at me but kept silent.

"This is a burn out and nothing more. I was far too infused with power from my link with Kwazeem and the Elohim's aura to collapse the day of the Festival," I argued, trying to convince myself as much as him. "As long as I remained close to Kwazeem, I felt strong, fueled by our bond. It's only once he left to hunt, and when I came back here that I faltered."

The dubious look in his eyes pissed me off, especially considering my legs were getting wobbly beneath me from trying to stand in a menacing stance before him.

"And if my Light has actually died, then so be it," I continued defiantly. "Kwazeem is my soulmate. All those years of training were so that I would come here to find him. I regret nothing. Whatever the cost, I will bear it gladly to be with him."

Frollo snorted and, standing up, he looked at me with disdain. "Such pretty sentiments, but oh so useless," he mocked. "You have two days to recover from this 'burn out' or be gone from here. If you are unable to perform the Chakra Ceremony, you will leave a holographic message with whatever bullshit apology you wish to spiel, and be gone not just from Paris, but from Eden itself. Hide in whatever Circle you wish, but you'd be wiser seeking an ally planet instead."

"You cannot force me to leave the planet," I challenged, feeling increasingly dizzy. "You may kick me out of Paris, but—"

"Do you have any idea what will happen if anyone discovers

that you are ruined?" Frollo yelled, shedding his cold and controlled exterior.

I recoiled and stumbled back onto the bed, gaping at him wide-eyed. Despite the shock, I welcomed being off my feet.

"Wake up, little girl! The last time this happened, it started a bloody war which caused the Fall. If the Elohim and the people find out another Anointed has been ruined, it will be open season on the Fallen. It will be a massacre. And I can promise you that there will be heavy casualties on both sides. So, yes, your skinny ass will get the fuck off my planet if your power doesn't come back."

I could feel the blood drain from my face for not having properly considered the consequences. Sure, people would be upset, but I couldn't be responsible for a witch hunt that would cause the deaths of hundreds of innocents. Defeated, I cast my eyes down, which seemed to calm him somewhat. He went on about how he'd forbidden Kwazeem to seek me out until we knew for sure if I was 'ruined' as he so eloquently put it. I didn't bother arguing or challenging him about it.

Whatever the outcome, I wouldn't part from my mate. With Vesta's blessing, I would perform the Chakra Ceremony in two days to eliminate any risk of unjust retaliation against the Fallen, bid my farewell to Paris, and then leave this planet with Kwazeem.

His speech done, Frollo turned around to leave.

"You don't need that case anymore," I called out as he reached for the door.

He looked down at the case held in his right hand before glancing at me over his shoulder. "Maybe, maybe not. Time will tell."

"I know what you've been up to," I said with contempt. "Bringing Kwazeem to the temple was never about protecting him, but to make it easier for you to exploit him. You've injected yourself with his Divine Light to become the most powerful ergokinetic human male."

Frollo snorted then turned around to face me. The undisguised admiration in his eyes as he gave me a slow once over took me by surprise. I'd expected a strong denial and self-righteous indignation.

"You're not so stupid after all. Such a waste," the Praetor said wistfully.

"You're not even going to deny it?" I asked, flabbergasted.

"Why would I?" he asked with a dismissive shrug. "He had something I wanted, and I could give him something he needed; a fair exchange. His Light helped me secure the highest position for a human on this planet, which in turn allowed me to give him as good and safe a life as his nature allowed."

"And what will you do once he's gone? When his Light fades from your system, people will realize you're not so powerful after all," I challenged.

Once again, he shrugged off my comment. "I have nothing else to prove and no one else to impress. I own Paris. In truth, I haven't used his Light in a long time except the day after your arrival. I did it to impress you because, unlike the previous Vestals, you hadn't rushed to my bed that first night to scratch that itch." Frollo took another step towards me, this time undressing me with a lecherous gaze that made me feel dirty. "That first morning when we had breakfast together, it had made you so hot and bothered for me that I could have fucked you right there on the dining room floor in front of the cook, and you would have begged me for more. If I'd known how you were going to throw away your future, I would have."

"You don't strike me as someone to deny yourself what you want. So, why didn't you?" I asked, my cheeks burning with humiliation at how wild with lust I'd indeed been that day because of Kwazeem's Light oozing out of Frollo.

"You don't publicly bend over the woman you intend to

marry," he retorted. "But, maybe if I had, we wouldn't be in this mess."

Without another word, he turned on his heel and left my room, the case still clasped in his hand.

∼

I woke up to the prickly feel of sharp claws hugging my face, and a small, hard little mouth kissing my cheek.

"Victus," I whispered, instantly guessing the identity of my tiny visitor.

Picking him up with both hands, I kissed his scaly forehead as I sat up in my bed. He beamed at me with his sharp, pointy teeth, then gestured towards my nightstand. On it, lay a beautiful bracelet with a stylized fire wasp on it, the symbol of the Fourth Circle—the moon I'd been born on. I marveled at the delicate and intricate work, enhanced by finely chiseled glowstones forming the shape of the wasp. I immediately realized Kwazeem must have started working on it the day we had our picnic when I'd told him about my homeworld.

My heart further melted for my mate. Getting out of bed, I hurried to the bathroom to wash the sleep from my face. To my relief, the weariness that had bogged me down all day yesterday appeared to have lifted at last. Fixing myself under the curious eyes of the imp felt a little awkward. We didn't have pets at the temple on Obscura, and this little guy didn't quite qualify as such either. Call me paranoid, but he seemed to enjoy the view a tad too much for my liking.

Once dressed, I settled at my desk to record a message for Kwazeem on a holocard. Victus made a nuisance of himself throughout the process, constantly poking his face in front of the camera, cuddling against my neck, and kissing my cheek. It was beyond adorable. However, that didn't keep me from getting the task done. As much as I ached to be with my man right this instant, we needed to play it safe and not needlessly provoke Frollo.

Despite everything, I didn't think the Praetor wished us ill, but he wouldn't go down for us. I put the holocard in a little pouch and gave it to Victus.

"Take this to Kwazeem. I'll see you all again either tomorrow night, or the day after the Chakra Ceremony," I said, carrying the imp to my window before kissing his little forehead between his horns. "Be careful and don't get caught."

Victus chirped, kissed my chin, and took flight after carefully looking outside for prying eyes.

The day dragged on interminably. In between failed attempts at summoning my Divine Light, I made sure to be seen by the locals, looking happy and healthy walking around the plaza and a few busy streets of Paris. Guilt gnawed at me as the people hailed me like a goddess as I passed them by. The atmosphere in the city was electric, no pun intended. Since the use of any type of nuclear or fossil fuel had been banned on most planets of our solar system, energy had become an even more precious resource. This made Vestals, especially high-ranking ones, national treasures that every Circle fought over. Now that I'd been here on Eden, I understood the extent of the First Circle's needs. They would be devastated. Their fury to have been given such hope of a brighter future only two days ago and have it already ripped away from them was inevitable.

I wanted to be their Vestal. I would without hesitation, but not at the cost of a life with Kwazeem. If only I could make them accept him...

*Assuming your powers come back, and that he isn't indeed draining you.*

Dwelling over such depressing thoughts was moot, though. However terrified I felt at the thought that I may no longer be a Vestal, there was nothing I could do about it but wait and see. To my shame, I had to admit that my bigger fear was that, should I indeed be 'ruined,' with time, I might grow to resent Kwazeem for it. He hadn't known the risks, but I had. Old Nan had warned me, but I'd stubbornly denied that possibility because how could the man I love be bad for me?

I returned to the temple to do a bit more research on which Circle might be most accepting of a human-Fallen couple, and then what other nearby planets might welcome us. For a brief instant, I considered approaching the Fallen tribes, first here on Eden, or maybe on one of the surrounding moons. Speaking to Old Nan, it had sounded like Kwazeem's mother had only been isolated for her child's sake and not because they'd rejected a hybrid. Now that he was an adult, would he still be so vulnerable to the Fallen's presence?

In the following hours, I put together an extensive list of questions to validate, and possible new places for us to call home. Thankfully, despite the embarrassment and maybe even shame that could befall my family once I'd left, the Temple of Vesta couldn't take back the dowries it had paid to them. Since I couldn't pack much of my belongings yet as it might raise the cleaning lady's suspicion, I spent the rest of the evening iterating on my farewell holographic message.

That night, I went to bed mentally exhausted but physically too tense to relax. Nevertheless, I managed to fall into a fitful slumber. Morning found me with a headache and a large gaping void inside me where my Divine Light had once been burning bright. This time, it finally sank in. I hadn't burnt out. I'd been stripped of my Light, of the tremendous blessing Vesta had bestowed upon me, making me unique, powerful, the light in the darkness that constantly threatened to engulf her children.

I was no longer a Vestal.

A first tear trickled down my cheek, soon followed by a second, then a third. A strangled cry escaped me before the dam burst open. I bawled helplessly, my body wracked with violent sobs as I mourned the loss of everything I'd ever been. My

Vestal status had defined me as a person and shaped my entire life. Who was I now? What was I? Would Kwazeem even still want me anymore? My Light had drawn him just like his had drawn me. Would he still be attracted to what was left of me?

I don't know how long I remained prostrate on my bed, my wailing having abated to a weak whimper interspersed with sniffling. A single hard knock on my door startled me. Without waiting for an invitation to come in, the intruder bypassed the lock and opened the door. I didn't need to ask who it was. Lifting my head, I looked at Frollo standing in the doorway. He held a stunning white staff in his hand that I instantly recognized as Kwazeem's work.

One look at my face drenched in tears sufficed for Frollo to get the answer he'd no doubt come seeking. A strange mix of pity, contempt, and anger flashed over his noble features. That cut deep and reopened the floodgates.

"Ever the optimist, Kwazeem gave me this as a gift for you to use in tomorrow's Chakra Ceremony," he said, showing me the staff before leaning it again the wall inside my room. "I told him you wouldn't get to use it," he added with a heavy dose of sarcasm. His gaze roamed around the room before once more settling on me. "Pack your things. Only bring the indispensable. The rest will be forwarded to you at a later date. I want you gone before noon," the Praetor said in a cold and emotionless voice. "My personal guards will meet you outside to fly you out. Do not forget to leave your holographic message in the Great Hall."

He pushed in the hovercart of food Malina had left outside my room, then left, closing the door behind him. Wiping my face with the back of my hands, I forced myself out of bed and gathered what few items I wanted to keep or might need on the new journey lying ahead. The sight of the trunk which had contained my ceremonial dresses triggered another wave of tears.

It felt too unfair, too steep a price to pay to be with the man I loved. Had following the desires of my heart been worth such a loss? As the question popped in my head, Kwazeem beautiful face appeared in my mind's eye, and a strange sense of peace settled over me.

*Yes. A thousand times yes.*

I wiped my face almost angrily with the back of my hand before completing my packing with renewed purpose. Any future without Kwazeem would be meaningless for me. So it was time to stop wailing over spilled milk. What was done was done. In time, I would recover from the loss of my Divine Light, but I could never recover from losing my soulmate.

After piling by the door the items I intended to keep, I finally gave into curiosity and picked up the staff. It was beyond exquisite. The white wood polished to look almost like ivory. Solid and well balanced, the intricate, woven patterns of the wood at each end of the staff were truly the work of a master artisan. Small glow stones had been embedded in a slanted circle around the staff near both ends. Covering the pattern with my hand, I gave it a twist and, as suspected, a sharp blade appear at the matching end of the staff.

But this was no regular blade.

Looking at it up-close, I marveled at the glowing veins streaking the dark metal. They appeared to writhe and heave like a living thing.

*Divine Light. Kwazeem's Divine Light.*

How in the world had he managed to infuse the metal with his very essence?

The sound of the trumpets resounding in the distance startled me, snapping me out of my mesmerized daze. As they continued to sound outside, it took me a moment to figure out they didn't come from the public entertainers that often cheered the crowd on the plaza. And then my stomach dropped at the realization they were heralding the Elohim.

*Why the fuck are they coming now? The ceremony is only tomorrow!*

Nearly choking with panic, I twisted the staff's pattern to hide the blade, grabbed the holographic disk containing my farewell and rushed to the elevator. As the lift raced down towards the ground floor, I prayed Frollo would meet up with the Elohim and keep them from coming anywhere near here while I made a run for it. But then I remembered he had magistrate engagements outside the city today. That meeting was also intended to serve him as an alibi as to why he hadn't kept me from running away once my disappearance would become public knowledge.

I tapped on the glass door of the lift, willing it to open the minute it reached its destination. The trumpets having gone silent outside meant the Elohim had landed. Going out the front door was no longer an option. I rushed towards the back exit, dropping the holographic disk with my farewell message on the altar near one of the two entrances to the chapel.

But I never made it to the back exit. The heavy doors of the main entrance opened, and the divine aura of the High Seraph slapped me with the strength of my impending doom. It drew me like a moth to a flame, the deep void that now gaped inside me hungry to be once more filled with Divine Light.

"Esmeralda!" Phoebus called out, his booming voice echoing through the empty hall of the temple.

For a split second, trembling with fear, I considered ignoring him and rushing out the building. But he'd already seen me. Even if I tried, there would be no way to outrun or lose him. He was the High Seraph, the military leader of the Elohim army. He always caught his prey.

I paused and fearfully turned to face him. With long, determined strides, he marched towards me with a broad smile, and a gentle, almost tender expression on his angelic features. He glowed with an aura of strength and power that seemed to suck the light and oxygen right out of the room.

As he closed the distance between us, his steps faltered, and his smile faded. The slight frown marring his forehead gradually turned to horror, and then into a seething fury. I took a couple of involuntary steps back as he slowly advanced towards me like a predator moving in for the kill.

"What happened to your Light?" he whispered in a dangerously low voice. "Who did this?"

"I… I'm just burnt out. It… will com-come back," I stuttered, backing away until the wall against my back stopped any further retreat.

"DO NOT LIE TO ME!" he shouted.

My ears buzzed from the deafening sound. Wincing, I resisted the urge to cover them with both hands. For a moment, I could have sworn the walls trembled. Continuing his advance, he invaded my personal space and brutally drew me into his embrace, his chest crushing mine. There was nothing erotic about the hold. His aura surrounded me, his Divine Light pushing into the gaping void in my chest, seeking my own Light to establish a link, a connection. But I had nothing to answer with. Unlike the day of the Festival when I'd already formed a bond with Kwazeem, Phoebus's power didn't hit a wall but passed right through me like the wind through an open valley.

The High Seraph released me as abruptly as he had embraced me. Visibly struggling to control his rage, he fisted his hands and spoke to me between his clenched teeth. "You will tell me who defiled you, and I will make him pay. The shame of a Fallen forcing himself upon you isn't yours to bear. Speak freely. No harm will come to you."

My lips quivering, I gazed at him with pleading eyes. "I promise you, Phoebus, I wasn't violated. There is no Fallen to be hunted. You saw the power I expended at the Festival. I'm merely burnt out from pushing myself too hard. Give me a couple of days, and all will be back to normal."

For half a second, I regained hope as a flicker of doubt

crossed his stunning features. And then he stiffened, his expression filling with a mix of disbelief and disgust.

"You consented," he whispered to himself, his glowing eyes flicking from side to side as he analyzed the situation before refocusing on me. "You voluntarily lay with that Fallen, and you're now protecting him."

"Phoebus…" I pleaded, clutching my staff with both hands and pressing it to my chest like a shield.

"TELL ME WHO HE IS!" Phoebus vociferated.

This time, I whimpered and covered my ears, fearing my eardrums would rupture. Curling up against the wall, I shook my head and whispered in a loop that there was no one. What patience the High Seraph still possessed snapped. I yelped when he caught me by the upper arm and pulled me after him. Without my staff, I probably would have fallen to the floor. My pathetic efforts to free myself failed miserably, and I half-stumbled, half-ran to keep up with him rather than be dragged like a dead carcass behind him.

His loud shouts had alerted the city guards, including Frollo's personal guards: Ulrich and Gareth. While the latter two stared at the scene with tense, knowing expressions, the other guards appeared utterly confused. Torn between their duty to protect any Vestal with their life and respecting the ultimate authority of the Elohim, they looked to each other for clues on how to react.

Storming past them, his fingers digging into the tender flesh of my upper arm, Phoebus exited the temple and bellowed an order at the two Archangels that had accompanied him—not his generals. One of them activated the interface on his armband while the other retrieved something from his weapon's belt. A hush descended over the city as the population looked on, mouths gaping and eyes disbelieving.

When we reached the plaza, a few meters from the Well's tower, Phoebus stopped and forced me to face him. Hypnotized by the bluish-white glow of his eyes taking on a reddish tinge, I barely registered the crowd gathering around us. With one hand, he tore my staff out of my grasp and threw it to the ground. He wrapped the other around my neck and, for a moment, I feared he would just snap it. But instead, he drew my face only inches from his.

"To think I wanted to put Elysium at your feet," he hissed. "Last chance to speak his name."

I pinched my lips and held his gaze in defiance despite the tears gathering in my eyes.

"As you wish," he replied with a cold, hard voice.

Phoebus cast a sideways glance at the Archangel who had removed something from his belt, before dragging me to the Well's tower still shooting a beam into the sky. The other Archangel approached us and, while Phoebus held me immobile, he clasped a collar around my neck. Deceptively flimsy in appearance, it could have passed for a black, leather choker, but it was as resistant as titanium. I stared in horror as he leashed me to the tower. The leash, an ultra-resistant and extensible silver thread, would only allow me to move around a two meter radius.

Humiliation washed over me as I stood, leashed like a dog, with every eye in the city on me. Phoebus released me and turned away, although remaining near me. The Archangel who had fiddled with the interface of his armband came to stand before us and released a tiny hovering sphere which I recognized as a camera. Blood drained from my face as understanding dawned on me.

Looking straight at the miniature camera, Phoebus delivered a message which I knew would be instantly broadcast on every media, throughout Eden.

"Citizens of Eden, I stand before you as your High Seraph and ruler of the Nine Circles. More than a century ago, Eden was plunged into darkness when the Light Eater Arahzor defiled the Anointed Vestal Armina, consort to High Seraph Galleus. That treachery initiated the Fall, the bloody war that raged for decades on Eden. And today, the same crime has been repeated."

A gasp rose among the audience who gaped at me with horrified looks.

"Only three days ago, Anointed Vestal Esmeralda brought infinite light to the realm, ushering in a new era of hope and prosperity," Phoebus said, gesturing at me. "But she's Anointed and Vestal no more. A Fallen has ruined her as Arazhor had ruined Armina."

This time, shouts of anger and outrage rose from the crowd, ready to turn into a mob.

"This crime will not go unpunished," the High Seraph continued, his voice filled with fury. "The culprit has until sunrise to submit to the Elohim's justice. Fail to surrender, and my legions will descend upon every Fallen tribe and clan on Eden until that animal is found and has answered for his crime."

My blood turned to ice as Phoebus gestured for his companion to stop the recording then turned to face me.

"You can't do that!" I pleaded. "That's not fair! There was no crime committed to justify the slaughter of innocents."

"No crime?" he hissed.

"There can only be a crime in the absence of consent," I snapped back.

Phoebus recoiled, and stared at me looking both hurt and disappointed. "So, you confess."

"I have nothing to confess. Love is not a crime. I am a free woman of the Nine Circles. I freely chose my mate and willingly accepted the consequences that might stem from it. I wasn't trapped, tricked, or violated. If being with the man I love means being stripped of my Light, then so be it. It is *my* choice. Not yours, and not anyone else's. Even knowing the consequences, I would make the same choice. I will always choose him."

The conviction in my words appeared to shake him. Until now, my heart had believed it, but my head had been clinging to what I had once been. But no more… I would always mourn the loss of my Light, but I could never regret finding the other half of me.

Phoebus leaned forward, his face inches from mine. "Let's see how honorable your mate is," he snarled. "He *will* stand before me and answer for this."

Without giving a chance to respond, he spread his wings and, with a powerful flap, took flight towards the temple, followed by his companions.

Falling to my knees, head bowed, I ignored the stares and murmurs from the crowd. Feeling helpless and defeated, I could only pray that Kwazeem would stay away.

# CHAPTER 15
## KWAZEEM

I watched the Praetor's private shuttle leave with mixed emotions. Although he'd come to see me get onboard with his personal guards, Frollo hadn't traveled with us to the Godswood. It had felt odd parting with the only person that had come closest to being a friend or family. I hated that I couldn't have personally given Esmeralda the staff I'd made for her. However, despite my somewhat tense relationship with Frollo, I trusted him to deliver it to her.

His meaning had been clear when he'd told me to keep it and give it to her myself. I almost agreed, too. But as much as I wanted a peaceful life with my woman, I didn't want her to have lost her Light. Or rather, I didn't want to have leached it out of her.

The last two days without seeing Esmeralda had been pure torture. I'd never thought missing someone could translate into literal physical pain. Even the power that had been buzzing through me had waned with each passing hour.

However, a different emotional trial awaited me now. Standing in the small clearing a short distance from Nan's house, my throat felt too constricted to swallow as I began to approach the house of my youth with hesitant steps. The small hovercart carrying my most precious belongings followed me with a discreet keening sound. The familiar scenery and scent had a million memories and long forgotten feelings flooding through me.

I'd often asked Frollo to let me come to the Godswood by foot to visit Nan. Until today, I'd always believed his arguments that it was too far away had been nothing but a lie to keep me under his thumb. But flying in the shuttle, seeing both the distance and perilous terrain I would have had to cross to reach it made me ashamed for having doubted his word.

Pulse racing, I closed the distance to the backdoor of the house, proud to see how well I'd reproduced its design in my cabin by the temple. My heart skipped a beat when the door opened before I'd even reached it. I then remembered the motion detectors Nan had put in place to protect me from unexpected visitors dropping by.

But none of that mattered. The beautiful, wizened face that I'd grown to love in my youth was all I could see. Her lips quivered while her gaze slowly roamed over me. My chest tightened at the love and joy in her glistening eyes.

"My boy," she whispered, opening her arms wide.

Tears threatening to choke me, I rushed to her and closed my arms around her frail body. Laughing and crying, she held me tightly, repeatedly calling me *her* baby, *her* beautiful little boy. I hadn't known my biological mother. Whenever I thought of home and of maternal affection, Nan's face always appeared to me. And in this instance, as she gently caressed my hair and kissed my forehead, I truly felt like the prodigal son returned home at long last. It worried me at first not to see my imps, but she quickly reassured me they had arrived earlier and were off hunting.

She ushered me into the house, and another wave of wonderful sensory overload assaulted me. Nothing had changed:

the same layout, the same décor packed with too many mementos acquired over the years, and the same delicious scent of freshly baked bread and sweet jams. Even my old room had remained untouched, aside from the bed which had thankfully been replaced by a much bigger one to accommodate my significantly larger frame.

Nan immediately began to fuss over me, making me sit at the kitchen table and piling a mix of every food I'd ever loved. I argued feebly that it was all too much, but I gladly gorged on every delectable morsel. There was something truly powerful about sensory memory. A familiar taste, a scent, a texture, and even the sound of the wind outside, each one triggered an onslaught of long-lost souvenirs.

We spent the next couple of hours catching up, or rather her grilling me about all that had happened in my life since Frollo had taken me away. Until now, if anyone had asked me about my life, I would have said it had been boring and uneventful, but as she further questioned me, I started seeing all that I had accomplished, learned, and experienced. My loft at the top of the temple's spire had given me a unique window onto the busiest city of the Nine Circles, and the best seat to watch all the grand spectacles often held on the plaza. Through my computer and vidscreen, I'd had access to infinite knowledge. Everything I'd ever wanted to learn about, Frollo had provided me with the necessary tools. Even my combat and blacksmithing skills, he'd provided me with top of the line virtual trainers. I'd hunted in the forest, went underwater fishing, and crafted the weapons of the City Guards.

"So, he kept his word," Nan whispered to herself, before locking eyes with me. "Through all those years, he gave you the best possible life for your circumstances. I'd been so scared that letting you go had been a mistake."

My throat tightened looking back at what my life had indeed been like. Remembering my last confrontation with the Praetor, a sliver of shame rose in the pit of my stomach. Frollo didn't love me, and I didn't love him. Yet, he had generally been good to me.

"He did," I conceded. "I missed you terribly, but you made the right choice." Judging by the immense relief on her face, she'd feared I'd resent her for 'abandoning' me all those years ago. "Frollo saved my life. We both know I would have died here had he not intervened when he did. Instead, he allowed me to grow into a man with the skills to care for a family."

A strange spark lit up in her eyes at that last statement. I squirmed in my chair knowing what question would come next.

"Do you love her?" she asked with a soft voice.

"With every fiber of my being," I said, my chest swelling with love at the thought of my woman.

"She seemed to have a great deal of affection for you when she came here," Nan replied carefully.

"She does," I confirmed. "We are… mated."

Her eyes widened, first with shock, second with joy, and then worry descended over her features. "Kwazeem, Fallen can—"

"I know," I interrupted, my stomach knotting again. "I mean, I didn't at the time, but I do now."

She blanched and pressed her palm to her chest. "Did you… Is she okay?"

"I… I don't know," I confessed, casting a concerned look towards her.

As painful as it felt to give her the gist of what had tran-spired, I was grateful that she would hear it from me rather than from Frollo. Still, being so far away from Esmeralda and not knowing her current status had me sick with apprehension. I wouldn't rest until she was out of Paris and by my side, or at least until I knew that her Light had returned.

We were deep in discussions about my possible plans with Esmeralda when the sharp, clinking sound of the city-wide alert resonated inside the house. Nan and I exchanged a concerned look, then she went to turn on the vidscreen in the living area. Before the image even appeared, my gut told me it wouldn't be good news for Esmeralda and me.

As soon as I saw High Seraph Phoebus, I jumped to my feet. A murderous rage slowly took over me as I watched my woman afraid, distressed, and leashed like an animal behind him.

"No, no, no…" Nan whispered before covering her mouth with both hands.

I didn't say a word, watching the whole message, my hands fisted so tightly that my nails started to dig into my palms. Only my self-preservation instincts kept my claws from jutting out, maiming me.

"I need you to call me one of those Vesta's Tear transportation pods," I said in a voice so filled with anger, it sounded like a growl.

"You can't go!" Nan exclaimed, jumping to her feet as well. Closing the distance between us, she gripped both my arms and stared at me pleadingly. "He will kill you the moment you set foot in Paris! Run away! There are places you can—"

I placed two fingers on her lips to silence her. "No, Mother," I said in a controlled voice. I hadn't meant to call her that, but my heart, not my head, was speaking right now. "I will not abandon my mate. And running isn't an option anyway. As we speak, security is locking down all the spaceports, and any ship trying to leave the planet will be scanned. I don't even have a ship to begin with, and Frollo will not put his neck on the line to help me escape. But beyond that, I will not be responsible for starting another war."

"I just found you again…" she said, choking up.

I cupped her beloved face in my hands and caressed her cheeks with my thumbs. "I should have died years ago, but I'm still here. It isn't my time yet," I said with a gentle voice, pushing my anger deeper down. "I, too, have just found you again, as well as my soulmate. I will not go down without a fight. You both have given me too much to live for."

"But Kwazeem—"

"I will *not* be deterred, Mother," I interrupted, gently but firmly. "Go on, please call the Tear for me."

She embraced me tightly, and her warm tears dampened the fabric of my shirt. I allowed it for a few moments. Thankfully, Nan spared me from pushing her away by releasing me. It broke my heart that I should have reentered her life only to possibly say my final goodbye. Still, if this was to be my end, I was glad to have seen her one last time and let her know that I loved her.

My imps returned from their foray in the woods seconds before the Tear arrived. They refused to be left behind. To my shame, it comforted me not to be alone in these last moments. After one last gut-wrenching embrace with Nan, I entered the Tear, carrying nothing but one of my staves. Thankfully, the autopilot took care of everything as I didn't know how to navigate one of these vessels.

A whirlwind of emotions coursed through me. Anger, fear, trepidation, and a sense of injustice all raged within me. And yet, beneath all of that, a strange sense of peace and acceptance kept me grounded. Despite the High Seraph's declaration on the streamed message, I still refused to believe Esmeralda's Light was gone. We'd been together the morning after we'd made love. Wouldn't I have felt its complete absence within her?

Halfway through the journey towards Paris, a flock of Elohim flew out of Elysium, all of them converging on my position. They'd probably been scanning all transports headed in and out of Paris to detect one transporting a Fallen. Despite the fear knotting my insides, I couldn't help marveling at their majesty as they flew in formation before surrounding my small vessel. Their powerful wings flapped almost in tandem with each other's. Their sole garment, a leather kilt, hid nothing of their rippling arm and chest muscles that screamed of superhuman power.

Each one carried a magnificent staff or lance. And yet, the petty thought that mine rivaled—if not surpassed—theirs still managed to cross my mind in this dire moment.

A couple of the Archangels turned to look at me through the windshield of the Tear. Their glowing pale blue eyes shifted to red to express their aggression before they turned back to look ahead. My imps whimpered in fear and curled up against me. Trying to rein in my own sense of dread as my vessel began its descent into Paris, I absentmindedly caressed their heads to soothe them.

The High Seraph and his small following flew out of the temple. They landed on the plaza only seconds before my Tear touched ground at its eastern edge near the stairs to the landing pad. Pushing down the terror that threatened to cripple me, I embraced the seething fury burning within me in order to face the challenge ahead.

The Angels and Archangels surrounded my vessel, leaving a single path towards Phoebus. He stood in the center of the plaza, holding his staff firmly planted on the ground, and my woman restrained behind him. Despite being clearly intimidated by so much hostility, my imps settled on my shoulders and clung to my neck. I couldn't tell if it was more out of fear of being left behind, out of solidarity, or a mix of both.

As soon as I stepped out of the Tear, the auras of the Elohim slapped me like a hundred hammers. I'd never stood so close to one of them before. For the first time, my Fallen nature—the Light Eater in me—awoke with dizzying force. My mouth watered with a rabid hunger to feast on all that raw energy. And yet, the power that Esmeralda had awakened in me, and which had begun to dim in her absence, also reawakened, surging forth, seeking what my body perceived as kindred essence.

Destabilized by these conflicting emotions, I looked at the Archangels towering over me with confusion. A similar expression temporarily replaced the murderous fury on their faces as I marched before them to meet the High Seraph. The crowd that had gathered around the plaza—although keeping at a safe distance from the Elohim's aura—muttered angrily upon seeing me. Some of the insults about my hybrid status and my hump, and the curses flung at me stung. Wearing a form-fitting shirt only emphasized my deformity. But knowing a battle awaited me, a loose garment would have only further impeded my already slim chances.

Despite the brooding expression on Phoebus's stunning face, I didn't miss the slight stiffening of his broad shoulders as I entered the radius of his aura. Even more than with the others, the High Seraph's power called to me. However, it was the Light of my mate I sought. I couldn't latch onto it with so much divine power surrounding me, muddling things. And yet, I could feel her.

"Kwazeem!" Esmeralda called out, looking distressed that I came.

Seeing her leashed to the Well's tower tore an outraged screech from Victus and Lazarus. All fears forgotten, my imps launched off of my shoulders and dashed towards her. Arrius and Magnus—Phoebus's two generals standing guard on each side of my mate—made as if to stop them but the High Seraph raised his hand in an arresting gesture, ordering his men to let the imps proceed.

They each landed on one of her shoulders, then kissed her cheeks before glaring at the collar. Grabbing it with their tiny claws, they pushed their magic into it. In seconds, the collar unclasped, releasing my mate. Arrius gasped in shock at seeing a divine restraint so easily discarded. Victus's head jerked towards him, and he hissed in a menacing way. Never breaking eye contact with the Elohim general, Victus glared at him and hugged Esmeralda's neck in a way that said 'don't ever mess with my girl again.'

Free at last, Esmeralda tried to run towards me but, lightning fast, the generals crossed their staves in front of her, blocking the way. She appeared to want to force the issue, but I shook my head, indicating for her to stay put. She hesitated before reluctantly conceding. Until I had a better sense of what would befall me, I wanted to keep her out of harm's way.

From the corner of my eye, I noticed Frollo's shuttle making a swift approach towards the city. But I dismissed it, having bigger issues to deal with right now. I stopped my advance a few meters in front of the High Seraph, feeling small in his towering presence and under his scrutinizing stare. I hated not knowing what he was thinking. Although still clearly angry, his scowling expression was lacking the seething fury and the contempt he'd projected in his message.

He half turned to look at Esmeralda and gestured towards me. "So, *this* is the mate you chose?"

"Yes!" she shouted proudly, lifting her chin with defiance. The crowd erupted in angry shouts, showering both her and me with insults. "It is MY choice!" Esmeralda yelled this time at the would-be mob. "I have filled your Well, as was my duty. That my performance exceeded your wildest hopes and dreams doesn't make me your slave or some broodmare for you to dictate who is allowed to be my consort. I have FREELY chosen this man. *I* pursued *him* when he tried to stay away for my sake. And now you are putting us on trial for exercising our most basic right of free choice?"

Pride and love filled my heart to thus be so unequivocally and publicly claimed by my mate. Her words seemed to shame a few among the crowd, but too many remained hung up on the cost to themselves of Esmeralda following her heart.

"You are not being tried for freely choosing your mate," Phoebus said to Esmeralda in a stern voice. He turned to look at me and pointed an accusing finger towards me. "HE is here to face justice for ruining you. Snuffing out a Vestal's Divine Light and destroying her ability to share it with the world is a crime punishable by death."

"I have not snuffed out her Light," I snapped, tiring of this discussion.

From the corner of my eye, I noticed Frollo skirting around the wall of Archangels to take position at the edge of the plaza. Tension plain to see on his face, his eyes flicked between Esmeralda, Phoebus, and me. But he had nothing to fear; I had no intention of betraying him.

"Yes, it is dimmed, but it isn't gone," I asserted with conviction.

"You would lie to save yourself?" Phoebus asked, his tone hardening, although he had spoken the words more as a statement. "None of us can find even the slightest spark within her. She's empty, completely drained of Vesta's blessing."

"If you feel nothing, then maybe you're not as in tune with the divine as you think," I snarled.

"You dare?" Phoebus whispered, eyeing me with disbelief.

Frollo frowned and imperceptibly shook his head. I ignored him. I was done with these games. The High Seraph hadn't summoned me here to have a pleasant chat, slap me on the wrist, and send me on my way. There was no point dragging this on.

"I dare and double-dare. I have come to face your justice. But, whatever the outcome, you will release my mate at once and *never* again hold her against her will, like an animal. As per your own laws, *none* shall ever harm, coerce, or otherwise mistreat a Vestal."

"Too bad *you* didn't remember that yourself," Phoebus deadpanned. Lifting his staff, he gave it a spin, his gaze never wavering from mine. "Defeat me, and you get to walk away from here with your life. Fail, and you will face my justice."

Blocking out Esmeralda's distressed face, I focused on my opponent. Calling up on my years of training—although limited to holographic opponents—I braced for what was to come. I had no illusions that I could defeat the leader of the divine horde who had walked out victorious of countless battles over the past century, but I wouldn't go down easy.

With dizzying speed, Phoebus rushed me. Our staves clashed with the deafening sound of thunder as I parried his attack. The crowd roared its approval. Like vultures, they wanted some bloodshed—*my* blood spilled for their amusement and revenge. Lightning erupted where our weapons collided. My arm muscles trembled from the force of the impact. But to my surprise—and his—I didn't stumble back. Standing my ground, I retaliated with a quick flurry of blows which he easily parried, although it put him on the defensive.

Turning the tables on me, Phoebus performed a roundhouse kick that I avoided by stumbling back. However, flowing into the rotation, he slammed the end of his staff against the side of my ankle, knocking me off my feet. I fell on my back with a loud thump. My hump violently striking the reinforced glass dome covering the Well sent a sharp pain down my spine. Grinding my teeth through pain, I barely managed to raise my staff in front of me to block a savage blow he was bringing down on me.

The crowd erupted in feral shouts, encouraging the High Seraph to obliterate me and crush my bones. The bloodthirsty cry didn't manage to bury Esmeralda's fearful shout. But I tuned them all out. If I was to survive this day, I couldn't afford any distractions.

After blocking a couple more of his attacks, I thrust the tip of my staff at him with all my strength, forcing him to back away. It gave me a small window to roll back onto my feet, spinning my weapon around me at the same time to keep him from knocking me back down before I'd regained my bearings.

We entered a battle dance, cycling through parry, offense, defense, feint, and dodge. Realizing that Phoebus wasn't going for a quick kill knocked me for a loop. He was clearly trying to inflict pain, but no mortal wounds. Was he trying to punish me before going for the kill? Was he merely putting on a show for those in attendance? Was he testing my skills?

Too many questions without answers, not that they truly mattered. But the more we battled, and the more the power that had gone back to sleep within me once Esmeralda left came back to life. I couldn't say if my mate's presence was provoking it or the heat of combat, but I welcomed it. As it coursed through my body, my strength and speed grew steadily. Instead of shocking Phoebus, a feral glimmer sparked in his glowing eyes, and a vicious smile stretched his lips.

*He'd been waiting for this. He had known this would happen.*

Out of the blue, lightning formed around his left hand, and he launched it at me. Taken completely by surprise, I stumbled back, not knowing how to parry this. The bolt hit me square in the chest with brute force. The impact hurt like a physical blow and made me slide a couple of meters backward. But to my shock, it didn't knock me off my feet and didn't electrocute me. The electric energy just glided over me like water on an oily surface.

An animalistic roar rose from my throat as something snapped inside of me. My power unleashed like a caged beast breaking free. Lightning erupted from my fingertips, and electric coils wrapped around my arms. The crowd gasped, and their heckling hushed. The bloody trouncing they had expected the Fallen hunchback to receive at the hands of their divine ruler now no longer seemed like an inevitable outcome.

Our surroundings blurred as I moved at dizzying speed, Phoebus meeting me blow for blow. It didn't make sense, and yet it felt as if we were too well-matched for one to get an edge over the other. Well… as long as he didn't use his wings. Just when hope began to blossom in my heart that maybe, just maybe, I would survive this day, the bond between Esmeralda and me reformed at last.

Timid at first, her Divine Light soared as mine rushed

towards her core through our link. The joy that swept through my heart and soul distracted me for a split second. But it had been long enough for Phoebus's staff to connect solidly with the side of my jaw, stunning me. Before I could react, a violent swipe at the back of my left shoulder sent me sprawling onto my stomach. The panicked sound of Esmeralda crying out my name drowned in the explosion of agony that nearly robbed me of consciousness. I all but tore my vocal chords to shreds screaming when Phoebus's staff collided with the base of my hump. My eyes rolled to the back of my head, and spasms shook my legs as I fought the darkness attempting to engulf me.

Grabbing me by the nape, the High Seraph, yanked me back, forcing me onto my knees. My body having ceased to respond to my brain, I couldn't fight back. He tore off my shirt in one powerful gesture, baring my hump back. Through the black dots dancing before my eyes, I watched the beautiful face of my mate drenched in tears as she screamed my name. The two generals held her back as she tried in vain to come to me.

An Archangel approached us, holding a gleaming sword in his hand, which he gave to Phoebus. I didn't know what the High Seraph had done with his staff, not that it mattered. In a moment, I would be dead. I only wished Esmeralda didn't have to witness it.

*Forgive me, my love.*

# CHAPTER 16
## ESMERALDA

Something snapped inside me at the sight of the sword being brought to Phoebus. I was going to fake fainting to free myself of the generals' hold when both imps attacked them, clawing their faces. Without thinking, I threw myself at my staff. It was lying on the ground, two meters away from me, where Phoebus had discarded it after ripping it out of my hand. My heart broke watching Victus get swiped by Arrius backhanding him, and Lazarus get zapped by a lightning blast from Magnus. Their little bodies flopped limply to the ground.

With a war cry, I spun around and struck Arrius twice with the end of my staff in quick succession. Although weaponless, he effortlessly blocked my blows with his forearms. Magnus grabbed me from behind, his huge arms around me immobilizing my own against my body. I threw my head back to head-butt him, but he, too, easily avoided my attack. Despite my combat training, I didn't stand a chance against two of the greatest warriors of the Nine Circles.

In desperation, I called onto the Divine Light I had felt resurging within me. Before Phoebus struck him down, Kwazeem had been fueling it, enhancing me again as he had in the past. I had hoped to get it a bit stronger than the tiny spark it currently was for fear it would fizzle when I first attempted to reveal it. But there was no more time.

Invoking all the power that I could muster, I unleashed a blast of ergokinetic energy at Phoebus. With both hands busy, one holding Kwazeem up on his knees and the other wielding the sword, he couldn't dodge or parry the attack. It hit him square in the chest. I didn't know what I had expected, probably for him to stumble back the way Kwazeem had when Phoebus had struck him with a lightning bolt, but not what actually happened.

Phoebus stared stoically at his chest where coils of electricity slithered over his chiseled muscles before fading away. He looked back up at me, an odd expression on his face.

"You cannot harm an Elohim with Divine Light. We are made of it," Phoebus deadpanned before turning his gaze back to Kwazeem.

"High Seraph!" Frollo called out just as I opened my mouth to plead for mercy now that my Light had returned. "My guards have informed me of what has occurred in my absence. I came back as soon as possible, but this proceeding had already begun. However, I and everyone else in attendance have just witnessed the Anointed Vestal Esmeralda use her Divine Light."

I held my breath, realizing he was fighting for us.

"She has," Phoebus conceded.

"It is common for Vestals to burn out after a Festival, which visibly is what happened in this instance," Frollo continued cautiously. "This hybrid can therefore not be tried for defiling a Vestal as clearly that wasn't the case. I also understand that he flew into Paris from the Godswood upon your demand. This means he didn't violate the trespassing laws forbidding Fallen to enter the city."

"That is also correct," Phoebus said, his face unreadable.

Although a little groggy, the imps stirring back to life struck me as a sign that the tide was turning. The Praetor was getting through to him.

"The Vestal is free to mate with whom she pleases. As the city's transport logs will show that she has previously traveled to the Godswood, likely to meet with him so that he wouldn't violate our laws, I am not sure what he is being tried for. This man has committed no crime."

"You're right. He is innocent of any crime," Phoebus said before his face hardened. "But I will finish what I have started."

As if in slow motion, I watched him hold the sword tip down like a stake and plunge it down into Kwazeem's hump before ripping it open. My scream of horror mingled with my mate's roar of agony. Kwazeem threw his head back and stared at the heavens, mouth gaping, before his eyes rolled back in his head. Through our link, a blast of divine energy knocked me to my knees. I yelled his name while staring numbly as blood and the silver fluid of his Divine Light poured from his back and pooled around him.

Through my eyes blurred by tears, I saw Phoebus hold Kwazeem's head up by the chin, exposing his throat. In a last surge of despair, I shot back to my feet to try and keep him from slitting his throat only to be stopped once more by the wretched generals.

But, to my utter shock, rather than giving him the killing blow, Phoebus and the Archangel that had brought him the sword reached for something in Kwazeem's back and yanked forcefully. My mate screamed again as dark wings matted in blood and silver essence protruded from his back, their tips held by the two Elohim. Reaching in again, they yanked once more, pulling out a second pair of baby wings. This time, Kwazeem's face, previously constricted with pain, dissolved in an expression of pure bliss.

I stood on wobbly legs, staring at him in disbelief. The generals released me at last, and I stumbled with uncertain feet towards my mate. Phoebus and his companion released Kwazeem who slumped while remaining in his kneeling position. Head bowed, hands dangling on each side of his body, he almost appeared asleep.

His stunted wings hung limply behind him, the white ermine duvet around his shoulders marking him as a Seraph, like Phoebus and his generals. My brain was struggling to assimilate what I had just witnessed, what it all meant. Falling to my knees before him, I cupped Kwazeem's face in my hands and lifted his head up to look at him. He seemed groggy, but his smile was genuinely happy, peaceful.

"Chant to your mate, Anointed Vestal Esmeralda," Phoebus said in a solemn voice. "Your Light will mend him and make him what he always should have been."

I gaped at the High Seraph who didn't wait for my answer before marching over to Frollo. The Praetor tensed but otherwise remained stoic.

"I know what you did," Phoebus calmly said to the Praetor. "Why you felt so familiar. You knew." Frollo didn't answer but held the High Seraph's gaze unflinchingly. "You will look after him in the temple until his wings are strong enough for him to fly to Elysium. We will deal with your indiscretion at a later time."

With these words, he spread his double pair of dark wings and took flight, followed by his generals. The Angels and Archangels—all white-winged—stopped before us, bowed their heads to Kwazeem, and then flew in formation back to their floating city.

Kwazeem's arms tightened around me, and his silver eyes began to glow with the Divine Light that had been trapped within him his whole life. My gaze locked with his, I began to Chant and watched his beautiful face take on a blissful expression. Lost in each other's eyes, I barely noticed our little imps coming to cuddle on our lap.

The Chakra Ceremony didn't take place the following day, or the following week. I had no interest in caring for the people who had so vocally wished a painful death for my mate. Anyway, my focus was on getting Kwazeem back up on his feet —literally.

My power had hurt Kwazeem in the past because it had tried to enhance what was trapped. Between my Chant and our link, his stunted wings grew at an exponential rate, to be as full and majestic as Phoebus's—which made them terribly heavy. One pair would have been hard enough to handle, but two was a true nightmare. I felt horrible for the number of times I laughed at my poor mate toppling this way or that. The funniest had to be watching him walk bent forward as if he was fighting a strong wind, just to avoid falling on his ass.

However, it wasn't just standing and walking that required relearning, but mastering this new weight distribution and balance while fighting, swimming, and blacksmithing. Sleeping also proved challenging for him. Worse still, he had to modify it each day as his wings continued to grow, taking up more space. Eventually, our favorite position ended up being yours truly lying on top of him with his wings wrapped around me like a blanket.

Shirts became a thing of the past for him, not that I minded the eye-candy. After years of living in hiding, it was difficult for Kwazeem to do the transition of walking around in broad daylight, his bluish-gray skin and scales exposed for the whole world to see. He didn't realize just how beautiful he was. While his hump had never bothered me, I couldn't deny loving how regal he looked now that he could stand straight, towering over us little people with his height of seven feet. Even Frollo looked dwarfed in my mate's presence.

Whatever tensions had existed between the Praetor and me

died that day on the plaza. We would never be friends, and I doubted I would ever genuinely like him, but an unbreakable bond would forever exist between us. Frollo wasn't what I would call a *good* man, but there was genuine kindness and loyalty in him. He had given a somewhat decent life to my mate for years, and tried to save him when others would have simply hid until the storm had passed. For that, he had earned my eternal gratitude.

The minute Kwazeem had landed on the plaza, the Elohim had felt his Divine Light and realized he was one of theirs. Because of that, Phoebus had immediately known he wouldn't kill Kwazeem that day. I wanted to punch him for having carried on with the charade regardless. He had deliberately dragged on the battle to force Kwazeem to use his Divine Light to reignite mine. Apparently, he'd felt my Light spark back to life upon my mate's arrival. As Kwazeem later found out the hard way while sparring with the High Seraph, Phoebus could have crushed him in a heartbeat with his eyes closed. He'd intentionally been going easy on him during the fight.

The kicker in all this? Phoebus was Kwazeem's uncle. The High Seraph's brother, Liantus, had apparently fallen in love with Kwazeem's mother while negotiating a peace treaty between their peoples, to reunite the Light Bearers and the Elohim on Elysium. But a war in the outer rings of our solar system had put the discussions on hold. As Liantus had died without revealing his secret, Phoebus hadn't known to look for a potential child.

It was no wonder Kwazeem's mother had been forced to flee the presence of her clan. As Fallen, they had hungered for the baby's Divine Light and had been draining his very essence. Unlike the Elohim of lower ranks such as the Angels and Archangels, as an angelic prince, Kwazeem's dark wings developed in a pouch that his sire would have severed between the ages of six and seven—a fact not widely known to outsiders.

Without his father's untimely death, my mate would have never endured all this pain.

Phoebus had wanted a harsh punishment for Frollo exploiting the boy Kwazeem had been but, to my relief, Kwazeem opposed it. As the 'injured' party in this mess, my mate made it clear that it was his call to make. I still had mixed feelings about Frollo's motives for intervening on Kwazeem's behalf during the battle. I wanted to believe it had been out of some kind of loyalty for my mate, but the Praetor was a practical man. Having a Fallen unfairly executed within the walls of his city would have no doubt started a major conflict with the other Fallen. There was no question in my mind *that* thought had crossed his.

Either way, we agreed that while the population would remain in the dark about the old gardener's true identity, Frollo would retain his role as Grand Magister of Paris.

Although we were welcomed to use my old quarters in the temple, Kwazeem and I ended up staying mostly in his cabin, making frequent trips to the Godswood to see Old Nan. It took nearly a month for him to be confident enough to perform the flight from Paris to Elysium while carrying me.

I would never admit it, but having a full angelic legion accompanying us during that flight alleviated whatever concerns I had that my added weight might make Kwazeem falter before reaching our destination.

Elysium exceeded even my wildest imaginings. Built around a series of floating mountains with lush, green plateaus, the city had been cleverly designed to almost blend with the surrounding nature while still using the finest technologies. No two buildings looked alike. Their colors, made to almost camouflage with their surroundings, still stood out enough to prevent you walking by without noticing their presence. With many structures built vertically along big elevations or giant trees, floating platforms could be found everywhere for non-winged dwellers. Today, that only meant the Vestals who had mated with an Elohim.

Light bridges connected the various floating mountains, only forming once you approached the sensors. It would take me a *long* time to become comfortable using them, if ever. Kwazeem was given his father's former dwelling carved directly into the mountain face with a stunning view of Eden below. Part of a large waterfall spilled into a private pond behind our house.

With huge reflective windows everywhere, walking around our new home felt like strolling on a cloud. While the artisans of Elysium would gladly provide us with anything we needed to decorate our house, what I truly wanted was the portrait of a beautiful hybrid boy holding a hatching imp egg to feature prominently above our fireplace. The next time I went down to Paris to perform my Vestal duties, I would have to pay Old Nan a visit and bribe her into giving it to us.

Thankfully not having any fear of heights, I stood on one of our balconies that gave onto nothing but empty air and a large forest, who only knew how far below. Kwazeem's powerful arms wrapped around my midsection. I purred as his teeth gently nipped at the tender flesh at the crook of my neck before kissing it better.

"Welcome home, my mate."

I loved the feel of his hot skin and the gentle scraping of his scales against my back. Turning around in his embrace, I caressed his back before my palms settled on the round mounds of his perfect behind.

"It isn't home until we've properly baptized every room," I said with a sinful smile.

Kwazeem's lips parted in shock before they stretched into a naughty smile. Eyes smoldering, he tightened his hold around me before brushing his mouth against mine.

"I can totally get behind such a plan," he whispered, his voice becoming gravelly with his burgeoning arousal.

While our tongues swirled around each other's, my fingers made quick work of opening the clasp holding his leather kilt around his waist. A single tug sufficed to make it fall down to his feet. Impatient to claim my prize, my hand slipped inside his undergarment to rub Kwazeem's stiffening cock. It jerked against my palm, and my mate growled his approval. The rippling ridges along the length of his shaft tickled my fingers as I gently stroked him. His hips began to move in counterpoint to my movements while his hands unclasped my cropped, strapless bustier top.

Fisting my hair at the nape, he tilted my head back to cover my neck and chest with kisses. As much as I liked to get my breasts fondled, I didn't let him get to his treat. Yanking his own hair back to make him stop, I pushed him backwards over the short distance to the wall. While my hand continued to stroke him, I kissed, licked, and nipped a path down his muscular chest. After a couple of short pauses, first to pay homage to the hard little nub of his nipple and then to tickle his navel with my tongue, I dragged down his undergarment with my teeth while accelerating the movement of my hand.

I got it only low enough to expose his balls before my mouth latched onto one of them. My free hand continued to strip him while I sucked on each of his silky, heavy sacs. Kwazeem's choked moan spurred me on. Dimmed specks of light sparkled beneath the skin of his testicles, their glow intensifying under my pursued ministrations. Just like everything about him, my mate was infused with Divine Light.

Moving up, my tongue laved and licked the ridges along his shaft before reaching the head and sucking it into my mouth. Kwazeem cried out, his hand tightening his grip in my hair as I bobbed over him. His aura swirled around me, slapping me with a sudden surge of lust. But *this* time, with *this* man, it felt right. And I gladly surrendered to it. With my nipples painfully hard and moisture pooling between my thighs, I slipped a hand between my legs to rub my aching nub.

Kwazeem suddenly yanked me up and, his hands landing

under my bum, he lifted me. I yelped in shock, and my heart skipped a beat when he carried me to the large stone railing of the balcony and sat me down on top. Fear and excitement surged through me as he dropped to his knees before me and lifted my legs over his shoulders. My mini skirt in no way prevented him from using his teeth to move aside the thin triangle of my thong.

I cried out as the burning heat of his tongue dove for my core. Head thrown back, hands fisting his hair, I moaned with ecstasy as he devoured me with rabid hunger. With half of my body dangling over the infinite void below, only his hands wrapped around my thighs kept me from falling. I should have been terrified, but all I could think was *more*. My hips gyrated beneath his sensual assault, and one of my hands let go of his hair to fondle my breast.

As if he'd heard my thoughts, Kwazeem stood up. His palms holding the middle of my back, he rammed himself home in one powerful thrust and swallowed my shout of pain with a greedy kiss. As he pumped in and out of me, the initial burn of his brutal possession quickly faded, soon replaced by waves of pleasure as the blunt head of his cock zeroed in on my sweet spot. The rippling ridges alongside his shaft enhanced each sensation a thousandfold.

I writhed beneath his relentless assault, hanging on for dear life. Fear and ecstasy mixed in a potent drug that had me speaking in tongues. A blinding light exploded before my eyes, and my mouth parted in a silent O as my body seized with a violent orgasm. Kwazeem cried out as my inner walls clamped down on his cock, squeezing him from all sides. Instead of making him topple over, it spurred him into an even more rabid assault. My mate pounded into me with such reckless abandon I feared the railing would break beneath me. But even as he was killing me with pleasure, I wanted more, meeting him thrust for thrust until we both fell apart, together this time.

And then the railing vanished beneath me.

I screamed as we fell over, seconds before Kwazeem's majestic wings began to flap. Heart pounding, I clung to him as he flew around the house to the pond at the back, his hips still pumping in and out, filling me with his seed.

The cool water of the pond felt icy cold on my feverish skin. Kwazeem swallowed my gasp yet again as he lay me down on a half-submerged, polished rock by the waterfall. My mate's hips picked up the momentum as he hardened again. Eyes glowing, an almost feral expression on his face, Kwazeem gave me a predatory smile.

"One area baptized," he whispered against my lips. "Now for number two."

By the time he'd finally taken pity on me, five areas had been baptized, with sixteen more to go. Welcome home, indeed...

# EPILOGUE
## KWAZEEM

"Thank you, Seraph Kwazeem," Mikku said with respect. "We will bring this latest proposal to the clans and get back to you promptly. Please know that we are tremendously grateful for your relentless efforts in finding a compromise agreeable to all parties involved."

"Elohim and Light Bearers were meant to live together," I said in a formal voice, although emotion tied my throat. "I am only happy to be able to help rectify this unfortunate situation."

"As are we," Mikku replied.

It was awkward to have my uncle address me with such deference. But as an angelic prince even the Angels and Archangels bowed before me. What a long way I had come from being the invisible hunchback of Our Lady of Paris.

It had never crossed my mind that the Fallen male who had called Old Nan for help with my mother going into labor had been her older brother Mikku. I had often wondered if I had any remaining family within my mother's clan. Finding that Uncle Mikku had secretly brought Victus's and Lazarus's eggs to Old Nan's shop for me had moved me to the core. In many ways, my imps had kept me sane through years of loneliness in Paris.

Along with the other three Fallen of his delegation, my uncle bowed his head before leaving the meeting hall of the temple. A year ago, who would have thought that four Fallen males—five if you counted me—would be publicly traipsing around the walls of the temple of Vesta in response to a formal invitation from the Praetor of Paris? Tensions had run high in the city when the first couple of visits had occurred. Today, they drew a healthy curiosity and a certain sense of excitement. The reunification of the Elohim and the Light Bearers meant the angelic auras would no longer be so potent as to negatively affect humans. That, in turn, meant the doors of Elysium might once more occasionally be opened to non-ergokinetic humans.

But for me, it meant reuniting the two peoples that I belonged to and completing post-mortem, the mission my father had initiated. It almost didn't happen. Phoebus's address threatening to raid the Fallen tribes and clans in search for me had rightfully angered them.

"Impressive work," Frollo said to me as the meeting room's door closed behind my uncle.

"Thank you," I said, more touched than I'd ever admit.

"You never cease to exceed my expectations," Frollo said pensively. "I still haven't found another gardener with half your skills. Forget about a blacksmith of rival talent. You snagged the woman coveted by two of the most powerful men of Eden. All of Paris bows before you in deference. And you are now mending a hundred year rift between the two dominant species of the Nine Circles. Good job."

My cheeks heated at the unexpected praise. Frollo had always been a man of few words where I was concerned. And yet, they couldn't have been more accurate than in this instance. But not only was I the diplomat that would reunite our peoples, I had also become the master blacksmith of the Elohim, with all my angelic brothers dying for a weapon crafted by my hand.

"I was raised with the belief that hard work yields rewards. It seems that was accurate," I said with pretend nonchalance.

It was the Praetor's turn to look somewhat uncomfortable. There was no love or friendship between us, and yet, that cold, selfish man held a special place in my heart.

Frollo cleared his throat and clasped his hands behind his back. "I never thanked you for interceding on my behalf when the High Seraph wanted to have me stripped of rank and exiled."

"Just like I never thanked you for intervening on mine when we all thought he was going to execute me," I deadpanned, holding his gaze. Frollo snorted and shook his head. "You took my Light to advance your career, take control of Paris, and become the second most powerful man on Eden. In return, you saved my life, gave me a decent life, and a proper education. We're even."

Although he tried to hide it, the Praetor's relief was palpable. Had he thought I held a grudge that might make me turn on him at a later date?

"I do have one question for you, though," I said, tilting my head to the side. "You knew from the beginning I was half-Elohim. The scan you did of my hump would have shown you my wings. Why didn't you tell the High Seraph?"

"Honestly, because I had no idea if he would welcome you, or kill you," Frollo said with a shrug. "And you alive was far more beneficial to me than you dead."

It was my turn to snort and shake my head. "Goodbye, Praetor."

"Goodbye, Seraph Kwazeem," Frollo replied, bowing his head with the proper level of respect.

Walking out of the temple through the main doors without disguise and without fear would never cease to thrill me. Under the admiring gazes of the locals, I spread my black wings and took flight towards Elysium. The wind blew past me in a cool caress as I journeyed through the sky with a sense of freedom in such direct contrast with my years confined in my loft at the top of the spire.

As I landed on the large terrace outside of our master bedroom, my chest warmed with love feeling the delicate aura of my son, Lucius. Making a beeline for his cradle where my imps were cuddling by his side, I picked him up, and he beamed at me with his adorable toothless grin.

In this instant, more than any other, it truly sank in. I was no longer the hunchback of Our Lady of Paris, a shameful secret to be kept hidden. I was the Seraph Kwazeem, son of Lantius, angelic prince of Elysium, master blacksmith of the gods, and unifier of the Fallen.

But of all the titles that had been bestowed upon me, only these two truly mattered: consort to the Anointed Vestal Esmeralda and sire of the young prince Lucius.

As I gazed upon my son cradled in my arms, I once more marveled at the perfection of his brown skin inherited from his mother, with golden scales around his neck and shoulders, and his silver eyes, identical to mine, staring trustingly back at me. He was the embodiment of the love I never thought one such as me could receive.

"Never doubt that you are worthy of love and happiness, my son. You are the living proof that love conquers all." I lifted my head to see my mate approach in a short, diaphanous, white nightgown. Extending an arm towards her, I drew her against me. "And your mother is the proof that as long you stand in Vesta's light…"

"…darkness will always be defeated," Esmeralda concluded for me. "I love you, Kwazeem."

"I love you, too, Mera."

THE END

ALSO BY REGINE ABEL

**THE VEREDIAN CHRONICLES**
Escaping Fate
Blind Fate
Raising Amalia
Twist of Fate
Hands of Fate
Defying Fate


**BRAXIANS**
Anton's Grace
Ravik's Mercy
Krygor's Hope


**XIAN WARRIORS**
Doom
Legion
Raven
Bane
Chaos
Varnog
Reaper
Wrath
Xenon
Nevrik


**PRIME MATING AGENCY**
I Married A Lizardman
I Married A Naga
I Married A Birdman
I Married A Minotaur
I Married A Merman

I Married A Dragon
I Married A Beast
I Married A Dryad

**THE MIST**
The Mistwalker
The Nightmare

**DARK TALES**
Bluebeard's Curse
The Hunchback

**BLOOD MAIDENS OF KARTHIA**
Claiming Thalia

**VALOS OF SONHADRA**
Unfrozen
Iced

**EMPATHS OF LYRIA**
An Alien For Christmas

**THE SHADOW REALMS**
Dark Swan

**OTHER**
True As Steel
Alien Awakening
Heart of Stone

# ABOUT REGINE

Regine Abel is a USA Today Bestselling author of sci-fi and paranormal romance. Anything with a bit of magic, a touch of the unusual, and a lot of romance will have her jumping for joy. Hot alien warriors meeting no-nonsense, kick-ass heroines give her warm fuzzies. Through her Veredian Chronicles series, Regine will take you to an exciting alien world full of mystery, action, passion and new beginnings.

**Facebook**
> https://www.facebook.com/regine.abel.author/

**Website**
> https://regineabel.com

**Regine's Rebels Reader Group**
> https://www.facebook.com/groups/ReginesRebels/

**Newsletter**
> http://smarturl.it/RA_Newsletter

**Goodreads**

http://smarturl.it/RA_Goodreads

**Bookbub**

https://www.bookbub.com/profile/regine-abel

**Amazon**

http://smarturl.it/AuthorAMS

www.ingramcontent.com/pod-product-compliance
Lightning Source LLC
Chambersburg PA
CBHW072017210726
48294CB00012B/840